MW00416052

Diversions

Diversions

Diversions

Hjalmar Söderberg

Translated, with an introduction, by David Barrett

Translated from the Swedish *Förvillelser*

Published by David Barrett
contact via www.onlineclarity.co.uk

Paperback ISBN 978-1-5153-8341-3

Also available as a Kindle ebook, ASIN B00M6FUK7U

The cover is adapted from a photograph by Carl Curman (1833–1913), a view towards Stockholm's Old Town and southern district, 1900.

Introduction

in which spoilers abound after the first five paragraphs

When in 1895 Hjalmar Söderberg entitled his first novel *Förvillelser* he was storing up trouble for any subsequent English translator, because the word lacks any fully adequate English equivalent. But his decision was a blessing for the translator who also wishes to write an introduction, because a little discussion of the choices and compromises thus required provides an excellent peg on which to hang a surprising amount of discussion about the novel itself.

A dictionary will offer 'aberrations' or 'errors' as translations of *förvillelser*, and it is true that these words contain the right echo from Latin, though heard only weakly in modern English: for the root of the Swedish noun is the largely obsolete adjective *vill*, meaning 'lost' or 'astray'. Then to *förvilla* someone is to cause him to become *vill* — in other words to make him lose his way, or, figuratively, to deceive or mislead him — and the act of doing so, and the state that results, are perhaps the earliest senses of the noun *förvillelse*, of which Söderberg's title is simply the plural.

English and Swedish are both Germanic languages, of course, and share many related words; indeed English too has an obsolete adjective, *will*, with the same sense as *vill*; and it has a closely related word that's still extremely common: *wild*; wildernesses are, after all, where we go astray and lose ourselves. Swedish also has this word (*vild*), as does German (*wild*); and it's likely that the same root gives modern German its word for wood or forest, *Wald*. So, forests — wildernesses — getting lost: all these ideas are tied together etymologically,

7

and perhaps the closest literal equivalents in English to *förvill-lelser*, sharing something of both its sense and its etymological heritage, are *bewilderings* or *bewilderments*.

But while those English words convey an innocent sense of (mentally) straying and not knowing where one is, *förvillel-ser* are not always mere misapprehensions or confusions. The characters in the novel, and particularly its hero or anti-hero, Tomas Weber, make moral missteps, and it is those that drive the entire plot. Indeed, this is the dominant sense of the word in the book's title, wilful strayings from the path of righteousness, and from this point of view a better translation of *förvillelser* might be *transgressions*. But that word connotes only a stepping over some threshold — all sense of lostness is lost.

Even a casual reading of the novel tells us that this won't do. Söderberg plays endlessly on the wider connotations of his title, and while there are no forests as such — the novel is set in Stockholm, after all — trees, bushes and the colour green stand in their place, amazingly abundant in an urban tale, a leitmotif of the wildernesses in which his characters go astray.

It begins with a green curtain hanging in the shop where Tomas meets Ellen; green furniture awaits in the room where their intimacy begins, with budding trees casting a green light across the couple's path there, Tomas's senses having already been addled by a brief encounter with some suburban trees; there are the watery depths of the mine, 'a greenish dampness, like the glint of sin', and of course the green-hued etching that saves the day for Greta in chapter fourteen, green orchids having hymned her progress to temptation all along. Examples pullulate; dreaming away on a midsummer afternoon, Tomas's sylvan cogitations run thus:

As far as the half-closed eye can see, the carpets of grasses stretch out in drowsy, even summer verdure; and summer-green trees with oddly crooked outlines stand motionlessly arrayed, like stage scenery cut half irregularly in some theatrical Eden. Elms, maples, chestnuts . . . and silver-grey poplars. And close by, at the very front of the stage, standing apart from the rest, is a large, green and very old ash tree. Beneath its canopy the shadow dreams dark and velvet-deep green. And there in the grass, isn't that something shining, white and tender, something that might be a woman's body? Something white and sleeping, turning softly in her dreams? It might be the first white and tender woman, Eve. It might just possibly be Ellen, or Marta . . . If only it were Marta!

And sure enough Marta then turns up, Söderberg not omitting to specify that the blade of grass with which she rouses Tomas from his slumbers is green. It remains for the reader to discover whether all this greenery has any transgressive effect on the young people concerned.

Söderberg's imagery is often more direct: the word *väg* ('way', 'path') and its inflected forms appear more than fifty times: people walk through parks wondering which way to go, a tree crashes over one pathway, prompting a change of route, whereupon someone points out that trees can fall on any path, Tomas is walking the 'Broad Way' of Matthew 7:13, Ellen, having taken the wrong path, finds it hard to turn back, the Lord sees people's ways, children's paths carry them from their mothers, who know not where they lead, and so on. Indeed, it seems the hero's principal activity is wandering the city streets, lazily straying this way and that. Lest we miss the point Söderberg finally brings his hero and heroine to an actual labyrinth — a maze, made of hedges of course — there to consummate their last happy day together. And, that note having been sounded, we are prepared for Tomas's dark night of the soul, when the cheery companionable streets of so many propitious encounters suddenly sink into a white anonymous twilight, a nightmarish labyrinth through which he dashes hither and thither, hunted and haunted, at one with the little stray dog he glimpses, in search of a way out of his predicament.

That he doesn't find one nicely subverts and thus perhaps redeems the one consistent narrative trope of the book which the reader may find dubious: for at all other times it seems our hero cannot step out of his front door without inadvertently running into someone and thereby advancing the plot; and occasionally, even in a fictional world, it really does seem too much — Tomas's final ('real') encounter with Ellen, for example. Still, at the risk of descending too far into the platitudes of the book review, it is fair to say that *Förvillelser* is generally a very accomplished novel, a minor masterpiece, even, published when its author was only twenty-six — and fair to add that perhaps Söderberg never quite lived up to its promise. In his later works *Martin Birck's Youth* and *Doctor Glas* — excellent as they are — Söderberg cannot always resist interpolating, not always seamlessly, pseudo-philosophical digressions that may occasionally seem ponderous or dated; in *The Serious Game* plot and character return to the fore, but the tapestry is much broader (fifteen years rather than the eight months of *Förvillelser*) and the threads more loosely woven. Thus this early work presents an appealing combination of lightness, concision and formal elegance its author certainly never surpassed and probably never repeated. We have noted some of the motifs that contribute to the book's structural unity, and the reader can hardly fail to be struck by the economy of many narrative choices. We leave Tomas and Marta, for example, in chapter five, 'shaking hands like two schoolmates making up after a fight' and begin chapter six somewhat jolted by the almost incidental report, dry but affectingly delivered, that their romance is in full swing; but on reflection we cannot be surprised, for the development seems to follow with near necessity from what we have already seen. This assured, elegant sense of when to cut into action and when to cut away creates, a little anachronistically, an almost cinematic feel: in chapter four, whose splendidly choreographed progress almost incidentally supplies the key to the dénouement, Tomas is wondering whether Marta is interested in him, and Söderberg gives us the answer with an abruptly striking cut amid many intentionally low-key ones a few pages later. And formal symmetries and cinematic metaphors come together when, at the very end, Tomas has a dream in which, unostentatiously but obviously, the film of the entire novel simply spools backwards to the beginning, tremendously compressed and bizarrely distorted, thus not only wryly echoing his melancholy reflections of the previous night, surveying the dreamlike pointlessness and incoherence of his life, but also foreshadowing his resolve to begin again. (His waking thereby becomes the very waking he contemplated, only effected rather more felicitously.)

Indeed, so formally compact is the novel that a number of minor characters struggle to achieve true individuality: their minute subplots are simply too sparsely strewn through the narrative for even the attentive reader to resolve as separate threads: they rather merge into a generalised gossamer sheen, like cobwebs on a lawn. Yet this too serves Söderberg's purpose, a sort of social correlate of his constant impressionistic sketches of the city or the sky, dabbing in the backdrop to his imagined world.

There are also missteps, appropriately enough: once or twice the author lets the reader down by delivering precisely the expected (and long telegraphed) 'surprise' (Marta's pregnancy); and, profoundly fond of his hints and symbols, he occasionally overplays his hand and they obtrude (the little girl's singing on Midsummer Eve; Ellen's cat scratch; the seashell, at once clumsy and improbable, that interrupts the otherwise quietly hilarious progress of chapter eight; Marta's autumn hymn); and sometimes we are unsure whether a device succeeds or fails. Tomas has all but raped the girl he loves, and who loves him, and then we are shown the little childish gifts they earlier gave one another lying abandoned on the floor: is this too much, is it mawkish and exploitative, or (even if it is) is it a tremendously vivid symbol of loss of innocence?

Because in this lies the emotional heart of the novel, whose excellences are far from exclusively formal or structural, and here the reasons for my choice of not-quite translation of the word *förvillelser* — 'diversions'. The word recalls games, played idly or unseriously, inattention and wasting time; it recalls wanderings and strayings; its greatest weakness (as a translation) is its lightness, its lack of any strong connotation of wrongdoing or error. Yet the transgressions and consequent bewilderments of Tomas and Marta arise at this moment in life when the ways of childhood, still so alive — and how telling it is to have Tomas revert to playing something like hide and seek with the girls as a formal dinner party winds down — find application for the first time to adult things, things not fully understood until it's too late: life is a game, and what are actually transgressions seem entirely innocent, diversions indeed, no more worrisome than a stroll in the woods. Hence the word *förvillelser*'s one appearance in the Swedish text, as Tomas's mother looks favourably upon her son's fondness for Marta and hopes that such an affection will *skydda honom mot många av de förvillelser, som nu för tiden fresta unga män*: 'protect him from many of those diversions that tempt young men nowadays'. Luckily for Tomas Weber, Söderberg was not, in the end, as cruel as his irony here.

D.J.C.B., July 2014

Diversions

(Förvillelser)

I

A young gentleman in a dark-blue spring coat and red gloves came out of a shop on Arsenalsgatan. The gloves were brand new; he'd just bought them in the shop.

He was very young, barely twenty years old.

It was one of the last days in April, an unsettled day, with the sky the blue of the sea and great flocks of clouds sailing overhead: an inconstantly smiling day, rapidly alternating sunshine and gloom and with keen easterly breezes blowing in from the skerries, from the sea. The bells of St Jacob's Church boomed and resounded: they were burying an old poet.

"Tomas, hello! How are you? New red gloves, I see . . . Congratulations on your pre-meds, I saw it in the paper yesterday. What have you been getting up to lately? I haven't seen you in days . . ."

This was Johannes Hall, a tall, dark-haired young man, six or seven years older than Tomas Weber. He had no real occupation and needed none, having some time ago unexpectedly come into a substantial inheritance.

"Well now, I did call on you both yesterday and the day before, but you weren't at home — as usual . . . Come on, why don't we go down to the Oriental and celebrate my exams with a bottle of wine?"

"Why not indeed . . . ?"

The streets were teeming. It was one of the first spring days, for spring was late this year. With every other step you encountered some swarthy, brightly smiling balloon seller with a colourful clutch of gas-filled rubber balloons. In the middle of the pavement on Karl XII Square was a group of children and teenage lads, mouths agape, all heads skywards as their eyes followed a red dot amidst the blue — a balloon cut free, sailing off over the rooftops.

Tomas walked on, smiling to himself.

"You're in a good mood today," remarked Hall, "has something happened?"

"Nah . . . well — I did just see a girl, in the glove shop back there . . . she had such shy, red-brown eyes . . ."

"Oh her! She's ever so nice. I've bought gloves there too, a couple of times. Both times I fell in love with her and resolved to do something about it, but then I forgot."

They'd come out onto Blasieholmen quay. Red patches of colour on the boats at the quayside shone in the sun. The harbour lay broad and blue and empty: traffic had yet to get into full swing this year.

"How old do you suppose she is?"

"I don't know — twenty-one, twenty-two . . ."

The Oriental was empty. Waiters glided like pale shadows in the gloom of the corridors.

Hall cast himself half recumbent on one of the low divans, whose colourful eastern fabrics gave the rooms their harem-like feel. Tomas Weber sat himself in a wickerwork armchair.

Sunlight flowed in as a broad, golden-yellow river through the window's multicoloured glass, with its yellow lilies and red tulips.

The silence dreamed on beneath the cornices' arabesques.

"Do you have anything to smoke?" asked Tomas.

Hall produced his cigarette case.

The wine arrived. You could tell from the stitching on the waiter's dress shirt that it was a costly thing. Tomas had received a fair sum of money from his father on account of his examination success and had no greater wish than to be rid of it.

Tomas Weber had an honest face with blue eyes and light-brown hair, which he combed back. His mouth, large but finely chiselled, expressed his powerful desire to take whatever life had to offer. He was of slender build and something under average height.

"You know what, Hall? I met Marta Brehm last night at the Mortimers'. We talked almost the whole evening about something I've now forgotten. How can anybody forget such things? She wore a white rose by her breast."

Hall smiled.

"So, is she still the love of your life? She has been for nearly six months now."

"Indeed, and I fear she will be for a good six more."

Hall nodded in distracted approval. He had a greyish, somewhat pockmarked face with a slender dark moustache, and he looked several years older than he was. His nose was angular, and his large brown eyes had a shifting gaze.

"I'm hoping she'll be at my table at the Arvidsons' dinner next week," continued Tomas. "You'll be there too, won't you?"

"I expect so."

Hall had been introduced to Consul Arvidson's family by the consul's eldest son, who was a close friend. He had otherwise few family connections in Stockholm. He'd been born in Brussels to a Swedish mother who returned to Sweden alone after a few years, lodging her child with a well-to-do artisan and his wife, a native Swede. At the age of twelve he ran away from his foster parents, and for many years nobody knew how, where or indeed whether he lived. Finally he turned up unexpectedly as an actor amongst a little Swedish provincial theatre troupe, and a few years after that his mother died, having first willed him her entire estate.

He'd made many friends and was widely seen in society. When Tomas asked him how he spent his days, he would reply: "I'm working on a drama. When once it's finished I'll hire a company of players and travel round performing it."

One pane stood open at the window. The salty spring air drifted in and stretched the cigarette smoke out into an airy net, whose frail dispersing fibres shone almost royal-blue in the shafts of sunlight. Outside, the coruscating play of light on the ripples in the harbour was so intense it almost hurt the eyes.

The wine sparkled in the glasses.

"Oh, by the way," put in Hall, "you're welcome to come along with me to the Opera tonight. I bought a couple of tickets for myself and Jean Arvidson, but he can't make it. Do you want to?"

"Of course!"

"That's settled then."

Hall emptied his glass slowly and filled it again. Suddenly he rose.

"I'm afraid I'll have to be off now. I'm meeting a friend at three. So then, see you tonight . . ."

"Yes. You'll be in at seven won't you? I'll come over to you."

Tomas stayed a good while longer, head heavy with wine and the spring air. Once more he found himself thinking of the girl in the glove shop. As she was helping him try on the gloves she had, a couple of times, stolen glances at him when she thought he wasn't looking.

Still the bells of St Jacob's resounded. From the site of the Royal Opera House came the sounds of hammers and the songs of the foundation diggers. Tomas drifted around in the human stream of the city, having neither cares nor goals.

On Fredsgatan he bought a bunch of violets from a little girl who curtseyed and smiled; then he went to a tobacconist's and bought a large, mahogany-brown cigar.

Wherever he turned he saw familiar faces; everyone was

out and about today. But if only he could run into Marta Brehm . . . She too, of course, would be out somewhere on a day like this: it was unthinkable to sit indoors. Where could he go that he might meet her? In truth the streets were empty that she didn't stride . . .

And then he suddenly recalled that she would most likely be wearing some new spring dress that he hadn't seen. Perhaps their paths had already crossed and he hadn't recognised her . . .

On Rödbodtorget he ran into his father, in lively conversation with a liberal politician. Professor Weber distractedly acknowledged his son's greeting with the same politeness he would have accorded any stranger's.

The waters of Lake Mälaren lapped green and white. A cutter with a crew of oarsmen and a patched sail headed out of the harbour with a perfect tailwind. The skipper sat astern, astride the tiller, and steered the boat with his backside.

Tomas had just decided to go up to the Karolinska Institute to see Gustav Wannberg, a fellow student whose company he often kept, to tell him he was busy that evening, when he unexpectedly encountered him under the railway bridge. Wannberg was a couple of years older than Tomas and had a head full of humanitarian concerns. On that day he was in a sombre mood because of the turn taken by the electoral contest in Belgium. Tomas walked up Vasagatan with him. At the corner of Kungsgatan they parted; Wannberg took his meals at a guesthouse nearby.

Tomas remained there for a moment, admiring the curious tableau down at the far end of Vasagatan, featuring the English church, a small, elaborately crafted toy of pale-red sandstone; directly behind it rises an enormous flame-yellow building with blue blinds at the windows, framed, seemingly in the same plane, by six dark, slender poplars. Taken as a whole the scene appears as a tapestry or a painted backdrop, erected across the middle of the road as a prank; and there is something oddly Japanese about its colours and contours that, by their affinity with the naively coloured woodcuts found in picture books, quickly captures a child's imagination when, taking his mother's hand, he makes his first excursions round the streets of his native city, and, many years later, returns it to his dreams at night.

A tram took Tomas back to the centre of town.

In the early afternoon the tide of pedestrians rose and swelled out over the streets and squares. Tomas stood hesitating outside the window of the glove shop he'd visited a few hours earlier. Should he buy another pair? They do wear out eventually, after all.

He was constantly jostled by people hurrying past heading for their dinner: he was in their way. He was all set to go inside when at that very moment the King walked past, in the company of General Kurck and the Keeper of the Royal Parks. The spring sunshine played and glittered in his beard. Tomas squeezed himself deferentially against the wall, hat in hand, and then went into the shop.

The shop was empty. It was dark, and Tomas was still dazzled from the sunlight outside. An old lady poked her head out from behind a green curtain and then directed a stifled call at some inner room: "Ellen! Are you coming, Ellen?"

The girl came out briskly.

"I'm looking for a pair of red gloves, size eight."

It was clear she recognised him at once. Her face at first expressed surprise, then she blushed deeply.

She was fairly well built, but she had slender arms and a slim neck. Her hair was rich, shiny and dark; her russet eyes gazed shyly. Her clothes were not particularly fine. On the left side of her neck was a slender scratch, as if a kitten's claw had caught her there; a tiny bright-red drop of blood was seeping slowly forth.

II

Tomas was drinking coffee in his room, as he usually did after dinner. With the coffee he smoked a Dutch cigar. His room was fairly small and furnished with some of the Spartan furniture from his parents' first years of marriage. The window looked westwards and the sun was shining straight in; it was getting on for sunset and the light was copper-toned already. On the wall opposite was the gently shifting shadow of a chimney vane from the roof across the way.

Tomas's mother was wandering round in the dining room tidying things; for a couple of minutes she stood in the doorway looking brightly at Tomas.

"Are you coming straight home after the theatre this evening, Tomas?"

"I don't know. We might eat out."

For a moment the room darkened. A dense cloud of smoke from a factory chimney had passed the window, driven by the wind.

"Tomas, is it really a good thing for you to be spending so much time with Johannes Hall?"

Tomas blew the cigar smoke out through his nostrils.

"Mother dear, I think I'm old enough to choose my own friends."

"Yes, indeed, I suppose you are . . ."

She went back into the dining room. Tomas could hear her dusting over the piano keys.

He started thinking about Marta Brehm. He had only to close his eyes to sense her tender girl's body gliding into the room, sinking down by his side on the couch and wrapping her arms around his neck. In a few years he'd be a famous doctor making twenty thousand a year; but just four or five thousand would probably be enough to get married. Oh those evenings at twilight, especially in winter, with the snow swirling round the street corners! He dared not even think about the wedding night . . . Marta would be presiding in violet velvet . . .

He might also go into politics — write articles in newspapers, enter parliament, maybe even become a minister. Indeed there was nothing in the constitution to prevent Professor Weber's son becoming Prime Minister. He could then find some position for Wannberg, something that suited his outlook and his abilities. And Hall too . . . which department was responsible for the theatres? Was it the education ministry? He could be education minister.

Out in the dining room the clock struck seven. Tomas emerged from his daydreams, quickly got dressed and was just ready to go when Greta, his seventeen-year-old sister, grabbed him in the hall and whispered, "Will you write my essay for me again?"

Greta was a fair-skinned, blonde girl with slender limbs. She'd been to confirmation classes the year before but still went to school.

"What's this one about?"

"'The Means of Grace'"

"Bloody hell — you can write that yourself."

"But if you did it, I'd see you got invited to Marta Brehm's party on Saturday."

"Big deal . . ."

Tomas extricated himself and ran down the stairway. The street lay quiet and empty; it was one of the broad, peaceful streets of Östermalm. In no time he'd noticed the substantial figure of his father a few steps ahead: he'd obviously gone out just before Tomas.

Tomas caught him up and accompanied him to the next

corner.

"Where are you off to?"

"I'm on my way to a shareholders' meeting. Afterwards there's a little games evening at the Karlbergs'."

Hall lived in a two-room flat on Kommendörsgatan. The outer room was very large, with three windows, and fairly sparsely furnished. On the desk there was always a blank sheet of white paper and a carefully sharpened pencil.

Hall lay on the couch dressed ready to go out. On a table by his head was a tray with a pitcher of Wynand Fockink curaçao and two glasses. Both had been drunk from.

There was a faint smell of musk in the room; a couple of narcissi lay abandoned on the floor.

Hall kept running his fingers through his hair, time and again, looking distracted.

"Well, okay then, let's be off," he said at last, rising some-what effortfully.

There was almost a full house at the Opera.

Tomas's heart skipped a beat when, during an interval, he spotted Marta Brehm's elegant, dreamy head up in the first tier. Who was she with? A chubby little lady with rich ash-blonde hair was leaning forward a little and talking to her, but a fan obscured Tomas's view of her face. Now she folded it. Ah, it was Mrs Wenschen! Tomas Weber went bright red with rage. Mrs Wenschen was no company for Marta Brehm!

"Good evening, Tomas!"

He felt a heavy hand on his shoulders.

"Gabriel, hello — is your wife here tonight?"

"Yes — she's sitting over there."

Gabriel Mortimer was a cousin of his mother's; Mrs Weber's maiden name was Mortimer. He was a man getting on forty, a government registrar. He had blue-grey eyes with an insistent, almost piercing gaze set in a rather frostbitten-looking face with large, well-defined features. He was wearing evening dress with a black tie.

In spite of their large difference in age Mortimer had struck up a sort of friendship with Tomas.

"Good Evening, Mr Mortimer, good evening Mr Weber — heavens, isn't it hot?"

This was a bald gentleman with something of the look of a tenor.

"I had lunch with the director of an insurance company and an artist, and afterwards we all went to Berns," he explained, apropos of nothing.

Tomas looked round for Hall, but he'd just gone outside to smoke a cigarette.

"Really?" said Mortimer with friendly interest. "Berns is indeed a very agreeable place. When I was last there — not very recently, mind you — a rat ran over my foot, and two others popped up a little way off."

The bald man laughed, embarrassed. Tomas excused himself on the pretext of saying hello to Mrs Mortimer. He found her in the midst of a lively discussion with an older lady dressed in black, on the subject of chicory coffee, presumably inspired by the advertisement on the stage curtain.

He exchanged a few words with her and then went out to look for Hall. He found him on the pavement outside the theatre. Tomas took him by the arm and they went a few paces up towards Blasieholmen Square without saying a word. The square lay quiet in the twilight, the evening sky vaulted blue-green and cold above them. One or two shadows moved silently in the half-light close by the walls.

A pale-faced teenage girl came out of a doorway, breathless; the door slammed behind her. She ran past, gasping, and across the square. She was burying her head in her hands and sobbing out loud.

"Why was she crying?"

"Yes — why *was* she crying?"

She was already gone, vanished down an alleyway — a slender shadow, sucked up and swallowed by the gaping darkness slumbering by the black-grey wall of Freemasons' House.

A stooped little man was walking around lighting the lamps, one by one, and high above the blackened masses of the buildings Venus was already shining, that brilliant flame of clear spring nights.

People were making their way to their seats again.

"Who was Mortimer talking to?" asked Hall.

"It was the gentleman with whom Mrs Helga Wenschen sought in vain to preserve her marital fidelity," elaborated Tomas learnedly.

"So, that was him . . ."

Hall's eyes followed Mr Wenschen with lively interest as, with a few strenuously agile bounds, he disappeared up the stairway to the stalls.

The chicory coffee ascended slowly amid the quiet overture.

In the row just behind Tomas one gentleman whispered to another, "Who's Mrs Wenschen sitting next to tonight?"

With a great effort of will Tomas did not turn round.

"I'm not really sure, seems to be some young lady . . ."

The orchestra blared. The popular baritone rolled on and began singing for all he was worth, dressed in his scalloped-edged lilac jacket.

It was packed out at the Rydberg. Hall, Weber and Mortimer with his wife and the old lady finally managed to cadge some seats in the depths of the great dining hall. The outer room was occupied by a meeting of veterinarians, who were concluding their conference with a formal dinner. An endless stream of waiters flowed back and forth through the restaurant; there were shouts, jostles and curses uttered through clenched teeth. Every now and then a sudden loud cheer came from the veterinarians.

Jean Arvidson appeared, wearing tails and a white tie; he'd been representing his firm at some industry function and now had a number of companions who looked like businessmen. He came over to say hello to Hall, Weber and the Mortimers; he knew them all.

He was strikingly pallid.

"You've been travelling?" said Tomas.

"Yes, back from Hamburg most recently, though I look like the dead of Lübeck . . ."

His health had been poor for some time.

"Well, no doubt we'll see each other tomorrow," he said to Hall, and went off in search of his party.

Seated by the wall opposite was a wealthy landowner, a member of the Upper House, yelling across the room that he wanted a pork chop.

Two gentlemen with a military air rose to leave from a neighbouring table; they shook hands with Mortimer as they passed. They were Gabel and Grothusen. Lieutenant Gabel was tall and fair-haired with a balding brow and a large narrow crooked nose. His trousers were almost scandalously elegant; they had tremendously big brash harlequin checks in black and light grey running obliquely, with broadly sewn seams down the sides. Gabriel Mortimer seized the fabric with unconcealed admiration; he bent down and lifted a piece right up under his eyes, because he was short-sighted.

"Where does your tailor live?" he asked.

"I'm not telling," replied Gabel with an urbane smile, at once flattered and offended.

Baron Grothusen was extraordinarily ugly, but he had a very handsome figure.

Tomas poured out some schnapps; it was Eksjö. He poured only half a glass.

Mortimer talked about Prince Eugen's paintings at the last exhibition; he was particularly enamoured of *The Old Castle*. His eyes followed Tomas's movements as he spoke; as soon as Tomas had put the bottle down he grasped it with a deft movement of the hands and without missing a beat of the sentence he had just begun poured himself a glass so demonstratively full it ran over.

A waiter carrying a large tray packed with glasses and bottles stumbled and fell headlong. He was only a young lad; he was fighting back the tears. The head waiter made a beeline. He had an austere, correct bearing, such as intimated that due punishment would be held over to a more suitable time.

The veterinarians cheered anew, this time rhythmically. Somebody had been giving a speech.

They'd arrived at coffee. Mortimer and Hall drank whisky, Tomas and the ladies Benedictine. Tomas had started to daydream. He'd abruptly been seized by a powerful urge to get a pair of trousers just like Gabel's. Hall prodded him: "There's a couple of chaps over there toasting you."

Tomas woke up and grabbed his glass. The gentlemen were Master Petersén and Dr Mentzer, two of his old teachers. They exchanged the little gesture which communicated that, for the time being, each approved of the other's bourgeois lifestyle.

The veterinarians' exuberance had reached its peak. They were cheering incessantly, and you could even catch sporadic attempts to sing 'From the depths of Swedish hearts'.

Mrs Mortimer began to yawn. Tomas felt a sudden prick of conscience — he'd forgotten to say goodbye to his mother before leaving. It was all Greta's fault, standing chattering about her homework.

Suddenly people were gathering round in the middle of

the room, and the hubbub subsided for a moment. An elderly gentleman had been taken ill and needed to be led out.

Mortimer, his wife and the old lady said good night and departed. Hall and Weber shifted their places round the table.

"That old girl can take her drink," observed Hall. "She downed three glasses in fifteen minutes."

The diners were thinning out. The veterinarians off in the outer room had broken up into smaller groups where dregs of conversation continued. Waiters paced around uncertainly like frightened sheep after a storm, pale grey, with dress shirts slack.

The two friends sat in silence. Tomas lost himself in dreams of walking with Marta in the still, summer air beneath the blue-green trees depicted on the mural tapestries . . . It was towards evening, and the pale stylised canopies of the elms were sighing coolly above their heads. In the otherwise empty foreground there stood a stone bench, the cold bench of loneliness and long reflection. Tomas and Marta had long since surpassed it, and deep in the forest, where the curving pathways petered out into a greenish darkness, a bird summoned with its long, delicate calls . . .

Suddenly the electric lights were turned off. A few gas flames were lit. The shadows played out ghostly wrestling matches around the walls, and through the glass panes, in the large green bar room where it was still light, a furious shadow theatre was performing, necks extended, arms gesticulating in the air with glasses in hand.

Hall sat quietly behind his tall, crystal-cut whisky glass, regarding the scenery. His face was forever unchanging. Any number of nights on the town no longer left their traces on this seasoned brow.

"Another day gone," he said, and threw away his cigarette.

Tomas closed his eyes. Ellen, the girl in the glove shop, had run through his mind. He couldn't stop thinking of her arms. It was Marta he loved, and yet it seemed to him that he would have forgone some substantial part of the pleasures life offered if he never set eyes on those arms, bare and white, reaching out to him from some dark corner of a room with blinds drawn down.

He shifted uneasily in his seat.

"Are you tired? Shall we pay?"

"Yes, it's late."

They rose to leave. Tomas went on ahead. The veterinarians' playground resembled a marketplace laid waste by some nocturnal hurricane. On a chair down by the door a waiter sat asleep, a young lad, crumpled like a rag. It was the one who'd fallen over with the tray. Hall patted him gently on the shoulders and slipped him a tenner. The lad got up, startled and confused, the perpetual bad conscience of the adolescent in his eyes.

"A little help to make up for that mishap with the tray," explained Hall discreetly.

"Well, are you coming? I'm ready."

A cold dawn light hit them from the square. At its far end the walls of the Palace rose ash-grey, uncannily large, that wonderful northern facade whose colours shift like the sea's. In the uppermost row of windows the brightening north-eastern horizon lit an array of palely green glistening opals.

Tomas had found a girl and accompanied her a good way along Regeringsgatan. She was big-boned and fat and had an honest if somewhat mannish air; it was clear at once that she didn't know the meaning of shame. After exchanging hellos they had nothing to say to each other. Tomas peeked at her shyly now and then. All of a sudden he made a sharp turn round some corner and shot off like an arrow down a side street.

He resolved to take the quickest route home. He was tired.

He walked as if sleepwalking.

A tailor with a pair of trousers over his arm came out of a little pea-green wooden house with yellow shutters.

Was he dreaming? Did tailors walk around with trousers over their arms in the middle of the night too?

Tomas exchanged a passing greeting with Justice Abel Ratsman, who'd just emerged from the same place. He'd met him a few times at the Brehms'. Ratsman was spoken of as a man with great prospects.

On Stureplan he found himself amid a group of revellers, a couple of whom he knew. He had to tear himself forcefully away so as not to be drawn along with the group, headed to some fellow's flat to drink cognac.

It was getting ever lighter. A pale sheen of dawn was already hovering over the drowsy winged horses on the roof of the Bång building.

On Sturegatan Tomas caught up with the tailor with his trousers. As he overtook him he turned and to his surprise found that it wasn't a tailor at all, but Baron Grothusen. Those were Gabel's trousers he had over his arm. *Where* had he come by them? He was walking perfectly steadily, and his pale frog face had the same assured, correct expression as ever. He was obviously under the impression that he was out walking with his own spring coat over his arm.

One leg of the trousers was trailing in the gutter.

When Tomas came in the front door he stopped, startled and surprised, at the sight of his mother asleep by the firewood basket, in her nightgown, a shawl over her shoulders. Next to her stood a candlestick with its candle flickering red, just on the point of going out.

She quickly rose from her slumber on hearing Tomas close the door.

"Ah, Tomas, you're home at last. I sat out here so I'd hear you when you came. Where have you been all this time?"

Tomas was cross. He wasn't a child any more. Would he never be free of this nonsense?

"Rydberg," he replied curtly.

He noticed she'd been crying and at once added more gently, "We ended up staying quite a long time; we had the Mortimers with us."

His mother grew easier hearing that the Mortimers had been there.

She got ready to retire.

"Is dad home?" asked Tomas.

"No, he isn't back yet, but I'm going to bed anyway; it was just you I was worried about. Good night. Oh, Tomas, you're too young to be out so much!"

She stroked his cheek, puzzled, almost embarrassed, with her empty left hand, and she retired to bed.

III

Tomas had no money.

He'd run through what his father had given him after his exams rather too quickly and didn't yet dare ask for more. Besides, his father had been sounding a little reticent lately when the subject of money came up. He played cards a lot and generally lost, though he was reluctant to acknowledge it; his clean-shaven, cherubic face always shone in the reflected glow of the winning party's quiet good fortune.

Could he turn to his mother? That would only cause her needless worry . . .

But on the other hand he could hardly go round with an empty wallet on these glittering spring days. He borrowed thirty kronas off Hall.

*

Ah, yes, the spring . . .

The boats down in Nybro harbour rocked softly as in a dream, their dark grey sails stretched out, because it had been raining overnight. The clock of Östermalm church struck nine. Tomas was out already. In a greengrocer's on Hamngatan he bought a punnet of German pears; he was planning to eat them in the shadow of an ancient oak out on Djurgården.

An empty tram rolled past; Tomas hopped on. A girl in a plain grey spring coat came running fast along the gangway. She clearly meant to take one of the seats in front of Tomas, but the speed of the carriage, which she made no allowance for, carried her instead to the seat immediately behind him. It was

Ellen; Tomas had recognised her at once. What should he do? Should he just sit there like a dummy the whole journey long, with his back to her? He quickly surveyed the scene. The conductor was busy elsewhere. He calmly rose, turned the moveable backrest of his seat the other way round, went over to the other side and sat down, opposite Ellen.

"Might I interest you in a German pear?" he asked, demurely and deferentially.

At first the girl, eyes wide with surprise, would have nothing to do with his pears, but after a little while she'd eaten two. Tomas respectfully handed her his visiting card, *Student of Medicine* set beneath his name.

She confided that she had business at a house at Djurgården.

The Bünsow building was brightly aglow with the sun, a glorious, unashamed courtly romance in stone. Tomas never ceased to admire the surfaces of these walls, in fact recent but which master craftsmen, contriving any number of irregular, barely perceptible modulations of the bricks' hues, had given the look of relics defying centuries of wind and rain.

Tomas tried to engage Ellen in learned conversation, but received only short, embarrassed replies. Meanwhile her limpid brown eyes wandered from his face to his cravat, from his cravat to the horse riders in the avenue.

They'd reached the end of the tramline down below the Hasselbacken. Tomas walked a little way with her; then she stopped abruptly and said, in a voice at once timid and ladylike, "I'm sorry, but you mustn't come any further. It won't do for people to see me in the company of a man."

Tomas blushed and bid a short farewell. He followed her with his eyes until she disappeared behind a green garden gate in the distance. Then he sat on a bench and smoked a cigarette.

The bars and restaurants on the square lay quiet and lifeless in the chalk-white light of the May morning. Tomas began to think about what he should wear this evening; he had, to the best of his abilities, written 'On the Means of Grace' for Greta and had indeed been invited to Marta's party. Should he wear a white dicky or a coloured cravat?

A covered carriage stopped outside the entrance to the Hasselbacken. A lady and a gentleman stepped out. Tomas smiled because he knew them: Mrs Grenholm and Dr Rehn, a prominent doctor. The spring sunshine softly lit the two old lovers' way.

A variety troupe of diverse races and nationalities passed by, cheerfully chatting away in three or four different languages. Their jesters' faces, jaded by late hours and makeup, cutting voices and gaudy, unkempt elegance came together in a colourful, exuberant dissonance that hovered in the air a few seconds and then faded away.

Once more the square lay sun-white and quiet.

Tomas rose and took a few steps. The garden gate in the distance opened again and someone came out.

Was it Ellen?

It was. Tomas's heart pounded and he walked slowly towards her.

Her eyes suddenly shone, seeing he was still there, and she blushed slightly.

"Forgive me," he said, with his honest blue eyes settled on hers, "but dare I suggest a walk in Skansen? If you have time."

"Well," she said evasively, "I really don't know..."

All of a sudden she remembered the bear cubs, which she adored.

"Yes. I'm free till midday," she replied.

And they walked together up towards Skansen. Tender new leaves were sprouting from the trees, giving a green tinge to the sunlight along their way.

Each spoke about their circumstances. Her name was Ellen Karlsson. Her father was dead; he had had a position at the Palace, and her mother now lived on a small pension. She had a brother who was seventeen and attended secondary school. He'd graduate next spring. He'd a good head and a great ambition to become a doctor.

Tomas was wondering whether he'd dare kiss her shortly.

They'd reached one of the paths edged with greenery that lead up to Bredablick.

No. Still too soon, but give it a quarter of an hour and he'd probably have kissed her. What then? Perhaps he could suggest dinner one evening?

The bear cubs were playing in their cage like puppies. The keeper had just appeared with breakfast: he gave them two large bread rolls each. He was carrying a deep tray with meat to take to the adult bears further along. The older of the cubs caught the scent of meat, and when the keeper took it away he started to cry, with an expression of such devastated despair that it almost brought tears to Ellen's eyes. There was something of the secret sorrow of the wild woods in his lamentations. He refused to look at his bread rolls as long as his eyes could follow the keeper among the trees. His brother, a more contented character and still innocent of such pleasures, had meanwhile gobbled up his own two rolls and immediately moved on to the rest. He might have saved himself the trouble: he got clouted straightaway, so hard he tumbled over several times. Bemused and crestfallen he walked off to the other end of the cage and lay down to sleep while the older cub, in a stifled rage, started munching on the bread. Halfway through his meal he recalled his sorrows once more and let out a howl that shook the whole of his shaggy body and gradually subsided into sobs.

Ellen and Tomas stared at the animals, captivated. Then their eyes met. There was no one else to be seen. The woods lay broad and quiet around them, and the wind hummed in the branches overhead.

Was this the right time?

She seemed to guess his thoughts, for her big red-brown eyes began to dart so anxiously, as if she were looking round for help.

"Let's go," she whispered.

Tomas abandoned hope for the day.

They came down onto Bellmansrovägen. He picked a spray of wildflowers from the wayside and fastened it by her bosom. He was happy to have hit upon this idea, unoriginal though it was, for his head was still spinning with the sylvan air and he was at a loss to know what to say or do.

Suddenly he had a new idea that was even better than the first.

"Aren't you hungry?" he asked. "I certainly am!"

She was not hungry, but he still persuaded her to come with him to Bellmansro for coffee and cakes.

They agreed not to sit outside, where they might be seen, and found somewhere in a little green-furnished side room with tatty seats, a table and a couple of chairs. The air inside was close. He helped her off with her hat and coat, and the waitress served them and left.

They drank coffee. A wasp buzzed by the window pane.

Tomas again noticed the slender reddish cat scratch, still there on her neck. But he couldn't take his eyes off her arms: these arms, naked, white . . .

"What time is it?" asked Ellen.

He wasn't listening. He snuggled up to her and whispered pleadingly in her ears: "Your arms . . . I want to see your arms . . ."

Tomas couldn't believe his eyes. For a few seconds she sat as if turned to stone, but finally, imperturbable as a sleep-walker, she took off her bodice and set it on a chair. Then she covered her face with her hands, bright red with shame. He drew her into him and kissed her everywhere — on her neck, her bosom, her corset. She sat as if paralysed; all powers of resistance had numbed in her young white limbs, and her shy red squirrel eyes flitted desperately around in fear and in horror. Suddenly she lost all self-mastery and threw her arms round his neck with a little shriek.

IV

Consul Arvidson was giving lunch at his villa by Humlegården Park, in spite of the advanced season. His wife was
turning fifty. Mrs Arvidson had been a beauty in her youth;
now, further on in years, she had acquired a striking resem-
blance to Karl X Gustav.

The long, spacious dining room had only two windows on
its shorter side; thus the hosts had turned day into night,
drawn the Venetian blinds and lit all the candles in the chan-
deliers.

The consul had just welcomed his guests. His face, near-
ing sixty, still bore that afterglow of youth which two bright,
ever searching, ever restless eyes can sometimes lend the
complexion of an ageing man of the world, itself faintly coloured by years of living well.

Colonel Vellingk sat at the hostess's side; the consul had
Mrs Weber at his table.

Tomas Weber's right-hand neighbour was Marta Brehm.
He had a sprig of violets as a buttonhole. He'd been with Ellen
every evening since Saturday and his head was dizzy with
happiness, though he was also a trifle pale. By way of explaining why he couldn't come to Marta's reception, he'd
spontaneously invented a story about a party thrown by a
fellow student to celebrate exam results, which he'd had to
attend for fear of making an enemy of him.

Marta had just asked him if he'd enjoyed this get-together.

"It was lamentably dull," explained Tomas plausibly. "I
was longing to get away the whole evening . . ."

Marta screwed up her eyes as was her wont and smiled

with ingenuous malice, as if she only half believed him. Marta Brehm was eighteen years old. Her willowy figure was slender as a sixteen-year-old's, but the play of her soft, assuredly balanced curves left no doubt as to her age. She was wearing a cream dress with long broad lace sleeves in which, with dream-like allure, the delicate to-ings and fro-ings of her maidenly limbs could be glimpsed. The neckline of her dress was rather high; she wore violets in her sash, and in her light-brown hair.

The Bordeaux was served, and they clinked glasses, smiling.

Opposite them sat Hall and Greta.

Greta was wearing her porcelain dress, as she called it. It was a bright, flowery summer dress with a blue and white pattern like old porcelain. At first her demeanour was somewhat prim, and now and then she cast a rather timid glance towards a large light-green orchid that Hall was wearing in his buttonhole, and whose peculiar shape almost frightened her. To her it seemed more like a living animal than a flower, some rare, light-shy creature of the oceans, newly dredged up from the greenest depths. As for Johannes Hall himself, she found him more ugly than handsome, but slowly came to appreciate his cheery, winning smile. They were soon getting on well together, and it wasn't long before Greta was behaving just as she would at home.

Gabriel Mortimer had, by one of those strange quirks of fate, been brought together with Mrs Wenschen, with whom he had, unbeknownst to any of the rest, once been on intimate terms. Their liaison had, however, been neither enduring nor serious. Mrs Wenschen was dressed in gold-grey silk and had a very low neckline. Mortimer peeked briskly down into her bosom with an indifferent expression, like that with which a tourist regards a landscape he's seen long ago and in which he's met with one or another insignificant experience. He was in a dark mood. What could he talk about that might be of interest to her? Suddenly he recalled the story of Gabel's trousers, which Tomas Weber had told him, and after only the first glass of the Bordeaux he'd related it to her. It was all the more suitable as Grothusen was sitting fairly close, diagonally across from them, and could serve as a visual prop for the tale. It put this vivacious lady into such a merry mood that it almost made Mortimer uneasy.

"Is that really so?" she asked, her confiding blue eyes stealing over to Grothusen with a melting gaze.

Baron Grothusen had no flower in his buttonhole, this being his first time as a guest in Consul Arvidson's home. He was conversing with Mary, the Arvidsons' unmarried daughter, about certain reforms in the military. He was especially keen to engage her interest in the introduction of dark buttons, of the same colour as the uniform; shiny metal buttons were obsolete.

"In the world of today they lend no lustre to our class but instead attract derision; and in battle they are quite simply dangerous. Besides, the measure should make a good impression in parliament . . ."

Miss Arvidson looked at him attentively with her serious dark eyes, which seemed always to seek out what was good and true in everything. There was a certain manliness about Baron Grothusen; something manly and dependable. And she observed, by the respectful courtesy shown by Colonel Vellingk as he drank with him, that he was highly esteemed by his superiors.

Professor Weber was with Mrs Brehm. It hardly seemed possible that this childlike little rococo pink head, its hair already white, should belong to a hardened and experienced woman, whose strong character had emerged safe and sound from serious crises. She had grown up in difficult circumstances, and her marriage had not been a happy one. She had separated from her husband eight years ago; he, a bankrupt businessman, had fled to America in the wake of various irregular transactions. She now received annual upkeep for herself and her children from her father-in-law who, besides being very rich, adored her. She also earned not inconsiderable sums on her own account from translation. Surrounded by her three children and a relative, Miss Berger, she was now living the happiest years of her life in a little flat on Döbelnsgatan. Apart from her father-in-law, who was a widower, the Webers and the Arvidsons were her closest and more or less only friends; her friendship with Mrs Weber went back to their youth.

The professor filled her glass now and then but did not make especially lively conversation; he was thinking about a little speech he meant to make. Gabriel Mortimer, her neighbour to the right, on the contrary engaged her animatedly on the subject of literature, which interested her greatly.

Mrs Mortimer sought in vain to initiate a learned conversation with Pastor Caldén, a middle-aged man with a bald crown and piercing eyes, whose dark priest's coat clashed sharply with the white shirts and bright dresses all around. He responded politely, but evaded all the great questions of human existence that the voluble Mrs Mortimer rained on his ears in such cheerful confusion. He would not be drawn into a discussion of what for him were the very highest things in a passing dinner conversation; and about trivialities he was absolutely incapable of talking at all. He therefore confined himself to concise, rather dry replies, and Mrs Mortimer could not decide whether they concealed the profundity of a wise man or simply a shy scholar's want of social graces. It was fortunate that the polite irony that in fact lay behind them escaped her entirely. Pastor Caldén was not a genius, but what he shared with the genius was that every sphere of thought other than his own seemed to him an empty shadow and an unreal game, because he had entered in to it and dwelled within it. He had

41

never known doubt, other than the sensitive man's doubt in himself, in his capacity and fitness to pursue some great task. The fervent ardour that possessed him, in the face of which every other consideration vanished like the morning mist, was on the point of taking him away from his modest work as a schoolteacher and turning him into a spiritual force, a force to reckon with, a ferocious opponent of the modernising tendency within the ecclesiastical world of the capital and of its foremost advocate, a very freethinking and highly popular priest who like a latter-day Absalom had been hanged by the hair between the heavens of childhood faith and the earth of common sense. Behind the iron self-righteousness with which Pastor Caldén championed his cause lay a deeper spiritual conflict than the world suspected. His housekeeper had more than once stood astonished, almost afraid, hearing his prayers coming from behind the closed door of his study: quiet, but with such an intensity that the wooden house creaked.

"How you've changed since you got married!" whispered Mrs Wenschen, directing a long glance of melancholy reflection at Gabriel Mortimer from behind her fan.

Mortimer had been married for over ten years, but in Mrs Wenschen's eyes was still a newlywed.

"Yes, indeed," replied Mortimer. "Especially from your point of view . . ."

She gave him a gently reproving kick on the shin with her little chubby foot in its glove-leather shoe. Her face had taken on a prim, almost offended look.

"Ow!" said Mortimer.

Mrs Wenschen sat with furrowed brows.

"Speaking of which," she resumed, "I don't like having Mr Hammer here. He looks like our guilty conscience."

Mortimer wasn't listening. He'd lapsed into contemplation, gazing out into space as he sometimes did. He had the expression of a man attentively listening to an anecdote at which everybody laughs, and of which he grasps every part except the joke itself.

Hammer was having a little difficulty keeping his lady entertained, Miss Dorff, a young singer. He was entirely unmusical himself and thus had nothing to say on the subject. Karl Hammer was employed in Consul Arvidson's office; he was, in addition, distantly related to him. He was a pallid man in his early thirties with fair, almost whitish hair and steel-blue eyes. Few now recalled that, some years before, he'd published a little collection of short stories of a kind that flung him headlong out of the esteem of polite society. He was twenty-something at the time and close to obtaining his doctorate, but abruptly broke off his studies for want of means and despondency over his diminished future prospects. No less unknown was the fact that he still wrote constantly, whenever his work permitted. In solitude his spirit had hardened. His secret ambition was to live among a select few who were truly dear to him, and upon whom he could lavish his affection, all the more cheerfully then to spray his pale, scathing contempt into the face of the rest of the world.

Miss Dorff helped him keep up the conversation with all the charm that forever stood at her disposal. She was, in actual fact, furious at having been seated next to someone of not the slightest use to her.

Grothusen, her neighbour to the right, was only occasionally able to accord her a few moments' attention. The regimental sense of duty with which he had originally approached conversation with Miss Arvidson was increasingly giving way to a genuine lively interest.

Mortimer had still not risen from his distractedness. He couldn't take his eyes off Tomas and Marta. Perhaps he was recalling something of his own youth, and its foolish and half-forgotten quest for an impossible happiness. Looking at these two young people, flushed with wine, heads bowed together, smiling and clinking glasses, eating one another up with their eyes piece by piece, his expression grew almost despairing. He seemed like a man brooding about a thing of indefinite value that he left somewhere, or dropped, or that was stolen from him . . .

"Bloody hell," he muttered through tight-clenched teeth.

What's more, he felt he was coming down with a cold.

Mrs Wenschen had found a soul mate in Johannes Hall, whom she'd just discovered sitting on her right.

Greta sat abandoned and a little downcast, rubbing at a small splash of wine she'd got on her dress. She quickly looked around, then neatly filched a pinch of salt with her fingers and sprinkled it on the mark.

Consul Arvidson and Mrs Weber were talking about young men's prospects these days. The consul's eyes had taken on such a gentle, wistful look, settling on Mrs Weber's already greying head, because once, long ago, there had been something, or a not quite something, between the pair: it was only a few kisses behind a garden wall, far up in the north, one Saturday evening in June, as the footsteps of the working folk tramped on the cobbles on the other side. In Mrs Weber's face and voice there was nothing out of the ordinary as she spoke to the consul about the competitiveness of the medical profession. Twenty years' marriage to a man she was warmly fond of had consumed her so completely that she no longer recalled her youthful crush. Time and again her eyes reverted to Tomas and Marta. She had noticed her son's affection for this young girl, and hoped it would protect him from many of those diversions that tempt young men nowadays.

Tomas and Marta were not saying anything sensible any more. They were stoked with wine and chattered about whatever came into their heads, and a great many things did. He was now telling a wholly improbable schoolboy tale, which gained nothing in plausibility from his considerable embellishments, and all the time his eyes were caressing her delicate figure, like a bowed stalk holding a flower, and the slow rise and fall of her breasts, and the folds of fabric over her delightful little maidenly middle. When the story was done he sat in silence: he'd chanced to think of that green room at Bellmansro . . . the quiet there . . . the wasp, buzzing in the window . . . He suddenly remembered that he hadn't, on that occasion, kissed Ellen on the lips, and a feeling of anxiety came over him, as when a young priest, long after the service is ended, is seized by the fear that he might have misspoken crucial words of the rite. Ah well, he'd subsequently made good every omission in that department . . . And once again his flitting thoughts returned to Marta. Did she care for him or not? And how to find out? Success had made him enterprising; he wanted the question resolved soon. And as he responded to her latest witticism with hastily assumed seriousness, his eyes clung to the meltingly carved line between her pale-red lips.

The champagne arrived. Professor Weber leaned forward and rang on his glass. He praised Mrs Arvidson's honourable life and proposed a toast to her. There was a good deal of feeling in his speech.

"Look at dad's Polar Star," whispered Greta to Hall. "See how it shines! I'm the one who looks after it and keeps it like that. It's stored with my necklaces and brooches. Dad wanted to keep it himself, in his desk drawer, but I wouldn't let him."

Hall's restless brown eyes preferred to settle on Greta than on the professor's Polar Star.

But in fact he saw nothing. He was thinking of an adolescent girl, fifteen years old, who had run crying across a city square one evening at twilight. She'd had a yellow-orange hairband in her slender auburn pigtail.

Why was she crying?

The toast was drunk to general enthusiasm. The mood reached its peak . . . the clinking of glasses, the tinkling of laughter, the buzz . . .

Tomas winked at Greta and raised his glass.

"The Means of Grace!" he said.

Greta reached out and clinked glasses with her brother across the middle of the table. She was choking back the laughter. Marta was in on the joke; she was holding her handkerchief in front of her mouth; indeed, she was biting it.

Farthest down at the end of one table Jean Arvidson was sitting with Mr Wenschen, the wholesaler. The ladies had left them. Jean was pale and silent. He'd suddenly started thinking about death. His doctor had indeed repeatedly assured him that the illness he'd borne for many years now was not in itself life-threatening, but still he could not escape the thought. He'd eaten and drunk practically nothing. The food nauseated him, and he fancied the wine smelled of iodine. A few green twigs, which had fallen onto the tablecloth from one of the bouquets, brought to mind spruce twigs and snow. To him the guests seemed like nodding Chinese dolls whose empty smiles had stiffened to skull-like grins. He felt a powerful need to get up, chuck his chair in a corner and be off, never mind where, just to get out through a door.

Wenschen drank his health constantly. He was in an excellent mood, spilled wine on his fancy tenor's shirt and launched one witticism after another. He was delighted at being left entirely to his own devices, sitting down there at the far end of the table and savouring the works of the Creator without any bothersome obligation to make conversation at all.

"Here I am, sitting at the end, sitting on my end, ha!" said he, and bumped his glass against Jean's.

He had a weakness for wordplay.

Jean laughed politely, but when he saw in Wenschen's face that he proposed to repeat his witticism so loudly that a couple of the ladies might hear it, he threw himself with passionate energy into a topic of conversation which he knew from past experience would interest Petter Wenschen: Bianca, the famous singer.

Now dessert was served.

"Here's to our old memories," said Mrs Wenschen to Gabriel Mortimer, not inconspicuously raising her sherry glass.

"Will you never mend your ways?" asked Mortimer anxiously, as he touched the rim of his glass to hers softly, almost tickling.

"I don't know," she replied fatalistically, her eyes coming to rest dreamily on Baron Grothusen, who in a momentary departure from the laws of propriety was stuffing three or four grapes into his mouth at once.

"I am, incidentally, not as depraved as you think," she added gently, almost gloomily. "Occasionally I get a little attack of remorse and sew a button on Petter's trousers."

Once more she gazed long and yearningly at Baron Grothusen, so long that their eyes met at last and for several seconds remained locked onto one another. He interested her. He was not handsome, of course, but he nevertheless made a very distinguished impression. Manly and distinguished . . .

Suddenly Mrs Wenschen was afflicted by a little fit of coughing, which necessitated sticking her fan into her mouth to maintain her bearing. She'd once more started thinking about Gabel's trousers.

And she whispered to Mortimer that the best part of all must have been seeing Gabel on the way home with two overcoats . . .

The ladies took coffee in the sitting room, the gentlemen in the smoking room.

The doors to the veranda stood open. Humlegården spread quiet and green in the dusk of the May evening.

Hall was leaning over the balcony railing and smoking.

He had found Greta irresistible and Mrs Wenschen stimulating. Otherwise he'd been fairly bored. It was an affliction of his: he could never let himself go, yield himself up.

She was beautiful and *she* was talented and *she* was charming and none of them was anything to him.

He was a rootless man.

It was ever thus, but he had not felt it as an affliction until that day when he found himself amongst the mourners, bent over the earthly remains of a woman, a stranger, who had bequeathed him her fortune.

In the days when he woke up in the morning not knowing where he'd spend the night life had at least had some edge, some excitement . . .

And he went back inside.

His eyes sought out Greta, but he found her busy with Mrs Brehm and Miss Arvidson.

Some of the gentlemen had sat down at the card table. Mrs Weber went past. The slight quiver of the hand with which her husband played out his last trump did not escape her notice, and she resolved to lobby the women for an early departure.

Mortimer and Karl Hammer were in a corner of the smoking room discussing Ritschlianism with Pastor Caldén. None of the three defended it, but Pastor Caldén attacked it from several different standpoints.

Consul Arvidson came past; he paused for a few seconds, listening to the conversation without himself making any contribution. He had not spent a great deal of time in thought, because he had lived a life without interruption, in a fugue of work and social obligations.

Mrs Wenschen, who liked cigarettes, had retired to a window niche with Grothusen.

Tomas came through the room.

"Where is Hall?" he asked.

Hall had left.

After a little while Tomas was playing *Run the Gauntlet*

with Marta and Greta through the whole house, including the kitchen.

Miss Dorff sang a few French ballads and one of Sjögren's songs. Mr Wenschen pressed in as close to her as he could, and when she'd finished he circled round her like the moon around the earth. The aim of his endeavour was to sing a duet with Miss Dorff. The odd thing about Mr Wenschen was that he really did have a very fine tenor voice.

Greta had sought out a secluded corner couch. She'd suddenly become so heavy headed, indeed, downright sleepy.

In a dark corner of the cloakroom Tomas and Marta stood kissing. He held her pressed hard against Mr Wenschen's Ulster and kissed her wherever he could. She was still as a lamb. The silly children had drunk so much champagne that they'd run out of things to say to one another.

A pause arose in the gentlemen's card games: they were telling anecdotes about Karl XV. Colonel Vellingk presided. The heat became ever more oppressive. The colonel looked for something he could unbutton or take off, but found nothing except the ribbon of his Commander of the Order of the Sword, bearing the badge of that order. He tore it off his neck and shoved it into a trouser pocket. And the old gentlemen remained sitting there a long time, their faces lit up equally by the wine and by reminiscence from that vanished time when a cheery and loose-living monarch peppered the nation's ears with legends of his licentious life.

V

Döbelnsgatan is that quiet, heavily shaded street which follows, on a gentle incline, the west side of St Johannes' churchyard. The smooth grey facades of the old houses loom untouched by the summer-green light that pours down onto the street through the churchyard's lindens and chestnut trees. In the old memory-filled churchyard itself, hordes of poor, pallid children play among the gravestones, climb up the balustrades and crawl up and down the broad stone steps in the sunshine.

Tomas was walking through the churchyard.

It was around six in the evening. The mottled brick spire of the church soared like a flame in the sun.

He'd not seen Marta since the meal at the Arvidsons', and that was getting on for a week ago. Every day in the late afternoon he would pace those streets where he'd most often seen her. All those pretty faces, known and unknown, that once would have captured his attention passed by as usual in the teeming city; but her he had not seen.

Where were her paths taking her? Was she keeping herself indoors? Was she ill? Then at last he remembered, hazily, as if recalling a dream, that at some point during the Arvidsons' meal he'd promised to lend her a book which had cropped up in conversation. He hunted it out and headed off to Döbelnsgatan.

The Brehms lived three flights up. In the gloomy entrance hall he fleetingly shook the hand of Justice Ratsman. Ratsman had been visiting and was just setting out on the way back. He had a short, fair beard and wore a pince-nez. He looked to be in fine fettle, although his figure was somewhat rotund.

Marta wasn't at home, nor was her mother. Tomas sat awhile in the old-fashioned little drawing room, whose finest piece of furniture was a very beautiful old dresser in empire style with a white marble top, and there talked to Miss Berger, whom he'd known as Aunt Marie since childhood. She received the book, gave it a brief evaluative glance and promised to forward it. It was *Heritage and Youth* by Jacob Ahrenberg. Aunt Marie was an old lady of almost seventy, but she still had a girlishly youthful figure and a pair of bright, gentle eyes. She had been a tower of strength for Mrs Brehm in difficult times and still managed the bulk of the family's household chores.

Tomas was dejected over his misfortune. What new stratagem could he now contrive to see Marta? He rose and conveyed his regards to the rest of the family.

On the stairs he paused a few moments, looking out of a window. Dust motes swirled in the narrow yellow-orange shaft the afternoon sun slanted in from the west. The little decorative red and green panes painted gaudily on the old-fashioned marbled walls, recalling the play of colours in a child's kaleidoscope. Silence reigned in the building and the courtyard outside, and beyond a languid afternoon calm lay over courtyard upon courtyard spread out before him. A towering windowless gable bathed its blind, empty surface in the sun's starkest sulphur-yellow light.

Tomas stood with eyes staring upwards at this eyeless wall. A heavy oppression had taken hold of him. How was it that he was standing here in the stairwell of a strange building, staring at an empty wall, unable to tear himself away . . . ?

Footsteps came from down below. A girl's footsteps.

It was Marta. She'd been walking quickly and was breathless and warm. She was wearing a plain dark-blue spring dress with something of red silk at the neckline. She blushed when she saw Tomas and then blushed even more, vexed that she'd blushed at all.

They greeted one another with a little embarrassment. Tomas explained that he'd dropped off *Heritage and Youth*. Then they stood in silence for a few seconds, unable to think of anything to say. He didn't know whether to address her as Marta or Miss Brehm. Taking courage at last he said softly, "I haven't seen you for so long, Marta."

"Tomas, you mustn't — Mr Weber, you mustn't call me Marta," she said anxiously. "You might forget yourself and do it where someone could hear," she added emolliently. Then she blushed again; it was surely a foolish thing to say.

But Tomas grew cross.

"Well, Miss Brehm," he shot back sternly, "speaking of proprieties, I regret I have neglected to thank you for your recent attentiveness. In particular I am most grateful for the amiability you displayed at Mr and Mrs Arvidson's."

Marta was close to tears.

"Yes but that doesn't count! My head was spinning so much . . ." Tomas couldn't help but smile. When Marta saw his smile she smiled too, with a tear in her eye.

"Look, Mr Weber," she said at last, desperately trying to seem earnest and sensible, "we're still so young, neither of us has any means."

Tomas had no answer. He stared in silence at the red and green lights from the window panes on the wall, and at the dust, twirling round redly and greenly in the shaft of sunlight. Seconds ran into minutes.

Finally their eyes came to rest on one another's.

"Are you angry with me now, Mr Weber?" asked Marta softly.

Tomas was silent.

"Tomas," she whispered, "are you very angry with me, Tomas?"

He took her hand and stroked it gently. Marta quickly looked around and in an irresistible urge to make everything right she offered him her red cheek, still no less warm now, to kiss.

Then they shook hands like two schoolmates making up after a fight, and they parted as good friends.

Once Tomas got down onto the street he started thinking about Ellen, whom he'd promised to meet at half past eight on the quiet and empty part of Strömgatan, outside the Bonde mansion. He should probably break with her . . . Now there was a thing . . . breaking up with Ellen! He considered the matter gravely as he walked up Döbelnsgatan, and he had not reached the corner of Malmskillnadsgatan before his pronounced aptitude for practical morality had recast this relationship as a kind of safety valve, which in his dealings with Marta would relieve him of every temptation — be it ever merely in fantasy — towards excursion onto forbidden ground. Besides, nobody knew anything about it, and nobody would ever find out.

Tomas went down the underpass to get to Drottninggatan by the shortest route. He wanted to drop in on Gabriel Mortimer to borrow fifty kronas. Sooner or later, of course, he would turn to his father with a request for the means of liquidating his debts — he might perhaps even be able to come up with some other reason why he needed money — but at the moment it seemed to him the time was not ripe. To be sure, he was no more intimately acquainted with his father's affairs now than ever, but he had nevertheless noticed, from certain small things, that they were not currently at their peak.

Tomas had recently discovered the concept of money.

Mortimer lived down in Klaratrakten. Tomas found him sitting at his big old mahogany writing desk, drawing funny little figures for his seven-year-old boy and colouring them in. The child sat with elbows propped on the desk and watched with wide, inquisitive eyes. Mortimer tried to unite the wholesome and the agreeable, making his drawings as educational as possible. He'd just finished drawing a crocodile and was now busy on a Chinaman. Beyond their geographical and zoological interest, these two creatures also served to illustrate two different uses of the letter C.

Whisky and water were produced, and Mortimer offered Tomas a very dark cigar, which he lit with a little hesitation.

Mrs Mortimer came twittering through the room. Over her arm was a little basket with socks that needed darning. Tomas conveyed greetings from home; this was from old habit — having not disclosed his visiting plans before setting out there were none to convey.

They talked about their plans for the summer. Tomas expected his whole family would stay in town, apart from Greta, who was going down to Scania to stay with relatives. His father might perhaps also make a short trip to Germany on academic business.

The Mortimers would be staying out in Dalarö as usual.

The child was scrutinising the finished drawings admiringly.

"Will you write a poem too, daddy, to say what the colours are?" he said.

Mortimer wrote a verse with big clear letters, and the boy read it aloud with the neat clear voice of an able child:

"'A Crocodile is green and grand of size;
Now let us draw with colours finer
A little Chinaman with narrow eyes
Down in the yellow land of China.'"

"China is yellow on the map," explained Mortimer. "It always has been; it was when I was a child." And addressing the boy he added, "Willy, go to your room and sit down and paint a little."

Willy went.

A red ray of sunlight played in the clouds of smoke in the room, and among the bronze ornaments on the desk. Out in the dining room was Mortimer's eldest girl, a little eight-year-old, tinkling away at an étude.

Tomas came to the point of his visit.

"Fifty?" murmured Mortimer, chuckling a little, "That's not pin money."

He took out a fifty-krona note, scrunched it up and tucked it into Tomas's shirt collar.

"You're walking the Broad Way, it seems," he added, somewhat more gravely. "Walk on, but watch out for the ditches!"

He paced back and forth in the room, a cigar in the corner of his mouth. As he came past the couch where Tomas was sitting he brushed him softly over the hair, as it were distractedly, without saying anything. Then he sank down into the rocking chair. He'd abruptly gone pensive and quiet. His face had assumed the same expression as at certain moments during the Arvidsons' lunch — an expression of brooding over something lost, something forgotten, or something he'd once been promised that never arrived.

It was half past seven when Tomas left Mortimer's. There was still almost an hour before Ellen was free.

Tomas drifted around.

The sun had already set and it was starting to go dark.

Gustav Adolf Square was bleak and deserted. Above the Palace the eastern horizon darkened to an ever deeper, denser violet-grey. It was one of those peculiarly quiet and muted spring evenings in Stockholm when the orchestras at all the bars and restaurants fall silent at once, as if by a flick of some hidden baton, and the source of the stream of flâneurs suddenly dries up and the last of the flow melts away into side streets and doorways. And in the very centre of the city you can stand for a long minute, astonished and alone, and listen to the sound of a carriage rolling off somewhere, many streets away, or look out over the square in wonder, letting your eyes follow the human shadows, silently gliding forth in straight lines through the twilight as if along invisible threads.

Then all of a sudden an orchestra strikes up and the lamps are lit, and the carts come rolling by and the flâneurs with their glowing cigars start to crowd the pavements, and once again you find yourself amid a living city . . .

Tomas had come out onto the quay at Blasieholmen.

White boats slipped in and out of the harbour with gleaming lights. The dark water fizzed up here and there in an ash-white spray.

He sat down on one of the benches in the stairwell of the museum. Just below him the human river was flowing along Skeppsholm, alternating sparsity and abundance from one moment to the next.

Again Tomas thought of Ellen. How would their relationship end? Her heedless devotion sometimes almost made him anxious. He would rather she saw nothing more in their liaison than he, a spring passion of young, urgent blood.

The air had grown misty, the gas flames shining through surrounded by big, reddish nebulae. Tomas stared ceaselessly at the faces filing past in the glow of the nearest street lamp. Already he felt himself a man of experience — of the world and of women — and he fancied he perceived the fervent, illicit dreams behind the long-lashed eyelids in every pale girl's face that the light of the flames lit up.

He looked at his watch almost every minute. Now it was nearly half past eight. Already Tomas seemed to feel the inviting, sultry air in that little out-of-the-way hotel room he and Ellen stole away to almost every night, and in which the broad, white bed took up nearly half the space.

The clocks had not struck ten when Tomas came home. Ellen dared not stay out longer — her mother would have been able to tell something was wrong.

The family was still sitting by the lamp in the dining room, all apart from Greta, who'd gone to bed. A place was still set for Tomas; he drank a cup of tea and ate a few sandwiches.

Before Tomas retired he looked in on Greta to say good night. It was dark in her room. He'd barely stepped inside when Greta came running at him, wearing nothing but a nightgown, and clouted him hard round the ear. Then she sprang into bed, burrowed her head in the pillows and started to cry. She'd got a D for her essay 'On the Means of Grace'.

VI

The spring passed.

On sunny days rain followed, and after the rain the sun came back. Spring costumes grew ever brighter and more summery, and the white narcissi withered and were forgotten for almond-scented bunches of cherry blossom and lilac, and the sun burned ever hotter on empty streets and houses with blinds drawn down, abandoned for the countryside. And the tender leaves on the trees in the parks grew and broadened into dark, deep-green vaults, in whose shadows weary people could repose and dream and trace lines in the sand.

The Mortimers moved out to Dalarö, the Brehms moved to a father-in-law's house on Lidingö, and the Webers stayed in town.

Tomas and Marta did not see each other often. Once they met when Marta came up to town to do some shopping; they went to a little out-of-the-way tearoom at the far end of Drottninggatan and ate cakes. But they vowed not to do it again, because chance ordained that they were seen by a friend of Marta's, who ought not to have seen them there.

Occasionally they also wrote little notes with disguised handwriting on the envelopes. They wrote nothing on these little notes, except that they loved one another.

*

The June days ran quickly by, like multicoloured pearls off a silk thread, and now it was Midsummer Eve.

Tomas had got up late. The evening before he'd been out

with Wannberg and a few other friends, eating a six o'clock buffet at Stallmästargården and revelling round in Haga and Bellevue the whole bright night long. On the way home a storm blew up and the rain came teeming down; he went with Wannberg up to his room, where they drank sherry and played chess. Outside the skies cleared, and the sun dazzled them when they put out the smoky lamp and rolled up the blinds. It was six before Tomas got home, and he didn't sleep much.

Around twelve he got up and ate breakfast. Once he was presentable he slipped a textbook into his pocket and walked down to Humlegården.

At the refreshment stall he ran into one of his companions from the day before, Anton Recke. He was a fair-skinned, dark-haired young man of fairly stocky build; he was a medical student of many years' standing, famed throughout his circle of acquaintances for his colourful love life and murky finances. His father was wealthy, but had tired of paying his son's debts.

They drank a few bottles of sparkling water as they talked over the previous day's adventures. Recke claimed to have ended up somewhere on the south side of the city, on Glasbruksgatan or some such. He lived in Östermalm.

He felt a little stiff.

Then he began lamenting that he had no money. Money, money . . . In his ears the word took on a mystical quality. It seemed he was standing face to face with something supernatural every time he managed to sequester a few banknotes in his wallet.

"Where do they come from?" he asked. "Nobody has ever been able to explain it to me."

He sat in silent contemplation for a long time, his eyes on the summer-blue sky.

"I only know where they go; but where do they come from?"

Tomas guessed he wanted to borrow money and offered

59

him ten kronas, being himself temporarily flush. Recke declined, politely but firmly.

"No thank you. When I want to borrow money I always let it be known right away. Besides, I left my watch with the errand boy a little while back and told him to bring the money here.

"Ah well, it can't go on like this forever," he continued after a melancholy pause. "A man has to find means one way or another. There's a brick merchant in Svartmangatan who's said to be helpful and accommodating . . ."

Tomas tried to persuade him to have nothing to do with dealings of that sort. Recke listened distractedly, preoccupied with calculations of his own.

The errand boy arrived with the money and a receipt. Recke emptied his glass and rose.

"I have to be at Wannberg's before one o'clock," he said. "I owe him Kr 2.65 from yesterday, and he said he had to have it before one today . . ."

Tomas stayed awhile with his sparkling water, watching the children playing in the sand; and he bought a few ginger biscuits for a little dog that came up wagging its tail.

A grey horse drove past pulling an ice cart. The horse had large sprigs of birch leaves in its harness. Only now did Tomas recall that it was Midsummer Eve.

And Marta had last written that she might be coming into town on Midsummer Eve to do some shopping. She'd probably be buying midsummer presents for her brothers and sisters; some little trumpets . . .

Tomas rose. He didn't know where he'd go, but he needed to move a little. He was afraid he might fall asleep if he stayed sitting too long.

Where might he find Marta? He had no idea.

He drifted slowly around the shadowy paths in the northern part of the park.

On a bench beneath an elder tree with green-white sprays of flowers there sat a very skinny old woman, hands clasped, squinting into the sun. A bottle of eau de cologne was sticking out of a greenish velvet handbag that had once been black.

She sat there nodding and squinting . . .

Tomas felt a powerful urge to sit just where the old woman was sitting, under the blossoming elder tree, sit squinting into the sun and looking out over all the velvet-soft verdure. If only she would get up and go! No doubt she'd been sitting there for hours. Did she have no curiosity about what the other end of Humlegården looked like?

Tomas went past her; after a few minutes he turned round and took the same route back.

The bench was empty. The old woman was tottering off down the path, propped up by her greenish parasol. She had a little dog with her now, the one that, a short time before, had come up to Tomas by the refreshment stall and got three ginger biscuits.

Tomas sat down under the blooming elder tree.

This is my lucky day, he thought. *I have only to wish for something, and all at once it comes to pass.*

It was serene and quiet. A dull echo of the hubbub from the streets and squares found its way here, remote and foreign, as from another world. The wind whistled to itself in the big old trees, the long drawing of a bow over a string, swelling, fading and dreaming into silence. Two yellow butterflies fluttered back and forth like living discs of gossamer paper, or the yellow petals of roses, torn by the wind from their stalk and driven to flight, to straying, wandering in flickering restlessness . . . And the wind never lets them find a lasting abode, and never grants them repose; it drives them together, then apart, and then together once more . . .

As far as the half-closed eye can see, the carpets of grasses stretch out in drowsy, even summer verdure; and summer-green trees with oddly crooked outlines stand motionlessly arrayed, like stage scenery cut half irregularly in some theatrical Eden. Elms, maples, chestnuts . . . and silver-grey poplars. And close by, at the very front of the stage, standing apart from the rest, is a large, green and very old ash tree. Beneath its canopy the shadow dreams dark and velvet-deep green. And there in the grass, isn't that something shining, white and tender, something that might be a woman's body? Something white and sleeping, turning softly in her dreams? It might be the first white and tender woman, Eve. It might just possibly be Ellen, or Marta . . . If only it were Marta!

And again the yellow butterflies fluttered before his eyes, rising and falling, converging and diverging. And the sky was blue and empty, and the wind hummed and faded, and all was quiet.

Tomas started. Somebody was tickling his lips with a blade of grass. Marta stood before him with red lips and smiling eyes and was tickling him with a green grass blade. Then she tooted away in his ear with a little tin trumpet.

"This is your midsummer present," she said at last, when she'd stopped tooting, and she handed him the trumpet. The gaudiest red and blue stripes ran round its bell.

Tomas and Marta walked together over Roslagstorg towards St Johannes' Church. They'd decided to go up to the flat on Döbelnsgatan and celebrate Midsummer Eve with a bottle of wine and some pastries, which they'd buy on the way. They dared not visit a tearoom — there was always the risk of being seen.

Tomas stopped in front of a stand selling toys on Roslagstorg. He wanted to buy something for Marta in return. Finally he settled on a little pig made of rubber. It was a special sort of pig: it had a hole in its snout through which you could make it suck up water; then you could hold it in front of someone's face, someone you wanted to amuse, and say, 'Look, what a funny little pig!' and when they leant forward to get a better look, you'd squeeze the pig round its middle and your friend would get a little squirt of water right in the face, which is highly amusing.

Such was the pig that Tomas bought for Marta.

They raced one another up the fragile winding wooden stairway that leads up to St Johannes' churchyard from Roslagstorg. When they were halfway up they had to stop and get their breath back. The ramshackle grey wooden houses on the hill basked in the hottest rays of the midsummer sun. The plants in the poor folks' windows twined their leaves and stems in yearning coils up to the dusty, rainbow-tinted glass. Not a soul was to be seen, only a black cat with white paws sitting on a threshold, lapping up the sunshine and relishing the midday heat with eyes tight shut.

Tomas briskly took Marta's head in his hands and kissed her.

They bought cakes in a little home bakery and a bottle of Madeira at a shop selling spices in Malmskillnadsgatan.

A dim, sultry light awaited them behind the drawn yellow blinds in the flat on Döbelnsgatan.

"We have to scare the ghosts away," said Marta.

She sat at the piano and played the clamorous first measures of Carmen.

Tomas tooted his trumpet.

"What will the neighbours say?" asked Tomas.

"There are no neighbours," replied Marta. "Everyone's left for the country. We're the only ones in the whole building."

She stopped playing, and neither of them said anything. A silence descended on the room like a house asleep in a fairytale. The old clock on the wall had stopped and regarded them silently and unblinkingly with its wise round face.

"What's in the packet?" asked Tomas, for the sake of breaking the silence.

"Presents for Midsummer," Marta answered distractedly, with wide, earnest eyes, as if she were thinking of something else. "Striped aprons for the girls, a necklace for Elsa, and this is for Johan: *The Amazing Adventures of the Nine Little Negroes.*"

They went into the drawing room. Marta pulled back the striped red dust sheet from the old-fashioned L-shaped couch; its pale-red fabric glowed faintly in the gloom.

"It's such a nuisance sitting on furniture with the covers on," said Marta.

She went into the bedroom, which looked out over the sunny courtyard, pulled up the blinds and opened a window. A square of sunlight fell into the drawing room through the open door.

Then she brought out a tray and a pair of glasses. They ate cakes and drank wine and sat on the couch reading *The Amazing Adventures of the Nine Little Negroes*. It wasn't a long book; they read the whole thing together in five minutes and thought it was great fun.

Then they sat in silence, looking at each other. They looked at each other for so long that it ended in a long kiss.

Through the open window in the bedroom came the sound of a child singing in one of the small flats facing the courtyard. It was the shrill voice of a little girl, singing a childish tune she'd made up herself.

Daddy's not at home now
Mummy's at the market
What shall we do . . .

And it went quiet again.

Tomas poured out the last of the wine, and they drank. The wine sparkled dark red in the crystal-cut glasses.

"Do you ever think about me when you're alone?" whispered Marta. "I often think about you."

He was playing confusedly with her watch chain.

"In the evenings, when we row out onto the water," she continued, "and at night, when I'm lying awake."

There was a tear in her eye. She softly wrapped her arms round his neck and kissed his hair.

Time and again she kissed him, his hair, his temples, his eyelids.

Tomas shut his eyes; he froze. He didn't know where he was. Was he dreaming or was he awake? His eyes shimmered, his ears whispered. He buried his head in her bosom, and his arms tied themselves convulsively tight round her waist.

In vain she tried to get up and writhe out of his embrace.

"No, Tomas — we have to go — it must be late already . . ."

Tomas didn't let her go. He was fired up with wine and wild with her caresses. She shut her eyes and sank back with a shudder and he took her stormingly, heedlessly, almost by force.

. . . .

Daddy's not at home now
Mummy's at the market —

. . . .

The dregs of the wine were glistening in the glasses.

Marta was holding a cushion to her face and sobbing softly.

"Go!" she whispered pleadingly. "Go, go!"

Tomas tried to comfort her, to calm her.

"I'm sorry," he said time and again, stroking her hand. But she just stammered out this 'Go, go!' over and over. It was as if she'd forgotten every other word.

Tomas went.

Marta stood in front of the mirror.

Was she the same as before? Or had she become someone else?

And tonight she'd dance round the maypole with the others, with her brother and sister . . .

She drifted back and forth through the rooms.

What time could it be? The boat would be leaving at four . . .

Marta had come into the little girls' room. On the wall there was a small cardboard shelf on which lay a piece of embroidery with the words *The Words of Life* in cornflower-blue silk. The shelf was covered with little red, blue, yellow and green slips of paper.

Marta chose a red one. She unrolled it and read: *The Lord sees your ways.*

All was quiet in the flats overlooking the courtyard. The little girl had stopped singing. Marta went into the bedroom, closed the window and drew down the blinds. Then she went into the drawing room to put the dust sheet on the couch.

The little pig and the trumpet lay discarded in a corner.

Suddenly she couldn't help smiling to herself: she was thinking of all those elderly ladies with nodding pointy hats who had sat lined up on this couch so many times . . .

The next moment she threw herself flat out on a cushion, crying so her whole slender body shook.

Tomas stopped in the middle of the churchyard.

Where should he go?

No, no that was not well done. But that he could have it undone . . .

He'd stopped in front of a headstone. He read the name and several titles, a year of birth and a year of death.

So beneath this spot, then, they'd buried someone who was once alive, and who now was dead.

Strange.

The church door was open. For a long time Tomas stood reading a notice to the effect that, in the summer months, the church was open every day from ten till three. Finally he went inside and sat down on a pew.

All the time he was pursued by the thought of this commonplace inscription he'd just read on the headstone: born there and then, died there and then.

Was that really true?

Then he recalled how a skull is always grinning. What is he grinning at? What right does he have, lying there all calm and peaceful, grinning derisively at the ones who are now out playing in the sun?

His thoughts had alighted on Ellen. Her image stood before him like a faded photograph, its outlines blurred, like someone he once had known, some other year . . .

Tomas had grown sleepy; the vaults were so high and so dark, and the organ was playing so softly . . . it sounded like sighing trees in a forest; perhaps it wasn't playing at all . . .

He himself had no idea how long he'd been sitting there when suddenly he startled at someone's touch.

A man stood next to him and was shaking his arm.

"The church is closing," he said.

VII

The cobbles burned under footsteps and the walls glowed white as ashes. The city lay in its summer torpor, drained beneath an Egyptian sky.

People cursed the sun and crept along in the shadows, wherever a strip of shade could be found, close by the walls or deep in the arboreal gloom of the avenue's edge.

All was quiet in the Webers' flat. The professor had gone to Germany, Greta was in Scania; Mrs Weber was sitting on the couch in her bedroom reading Thomas à Kempis and crying. Occasionally she would, quite suddenly, feel so lonely and abandoned there in the midst of her family that she knew no other recourse than to cry. Her children were growing away from her. What did she know of the paths they were taking? A shudder of dread ran through her every time she considered all the evil the next day, or the next year might hold in store for us, without our knowing or being able to do anything about it. It may be that the seed was already sown — perhaps yesterday, perhaps the day before yesterday, or perhaps on some un-known, unhappy day long ago — and was now growing in silence, one day to sprout up with poisonous flowers and black-green berries . . . But Tomas was lying on the couch in his room. He'd pulled down the blinds even though it was mid-morning and his window lay in shadow, because the wall opposite glared and stung his eyes with its white sea of fire. The book he'd recently taken down from the shelf had lapsed onto the floor. He couldn't read.

Marta . . .

What was she thinking about him? What was her opinion

of him? Time and again he'd sat down to write to her, and he'd pondered and brooded and found no words. And when at last he had finished a letter, full of remorse and bitter self-reproaches, he read it through, once, twice over, sealed it in an envelope, tore open the envelope and read it again and burned it in a candle.

What kind of day was she having?

Was she reading, sewing as before, playing with her siblings? And what did she talk about with her family?

Noise from the street crowded in through the open window. It was a clatter as if every last brewery cart in hell was commanded to drive back and forth all day long on precisely this backstreet.

Tomas got up and shut the window; then he threw himself back on the couch.

Maybe she walked alone in the woods all day long, every day. And at night . . . did she get up in the night, walk out onto the jetty and stand there, staring down into the water?

How many days was it now since Midsummer Eve? Five days, or six. Almost a week.

He'd grown a little embarrassed when she'd asked him whether he often thought about her. He was well aware that he thought more about Ellen than about her. That was then . . . Now he thought about her continually, constantly.

Ellen he had forgotten.

Poor Ellen. He'd not done right by her.

The flies buzzed around his head and danced in a maze of zigzags before his eyes. Perhaps they were the little black souls of wicked, stupid people, condemned to buzz round and plague the wicked, stupid people now inhabiting the world. A fitting contrivance that would be for a wicked, stupid god . . .

They were creeping in his ears and tickling the corners of his mouth, and one sat on his nose, washing its back legs.

Tomas went out into the kitchen looking for the net to

catch them in and then started on a frenzied hunt. He tired of it after a few minutes, shook the flies out of the window and lay back down again.

All his beautiful dreams of winter evenings before the fire, his head in her lap — polluted, ruined, gone!

And the wedding night . . . He was forever taking things on tick . . . It wasn't right; one should never do that.

And never again would she smile at him and wrap her arms around his neck and kiss his eyelids and call him sweet names that he didn't deserve, but which it was nice to hear anyway.

He bit into the pillow under his head, and the worn silk cover came apart and he got a mouthful of down and feather. He turned to the wall, enervated by the heat of the room, and let his eyes roam wearily along the narrow channels among the wallpaper's arabesques, until his eyes felt the same yearning for a wide, bright surface as the sailor for the sea.

The sea . . . it was a long time since he'd seen the sea.

The vast, blue sea.

Tomas walked irresolutely up and down Blasieholmen quay. He longed to breathe salt air. Which boat should he choose?

A gentleman in a great hurry greeted him warmly. Tomas responded politely and distractedly. It was Justice Ratsman; he looked plump and happy and wore a bright cravat, and he got aboard the Lidingö boat just as it put out. He didn't live on Lidingö, but in Vaxholm, but he was probably going to visit friends . . .

Tomas had come to a halt in front of a small old-fashioned sooty steamboat. It was called the *Far Isle*, and it was to Far Isle that it would depart in fifteen minutes' time.

Far Isle — that sounded as if it should be right out by the sea . . .

He wrote a few lines to his mother and handed them to a messenger boy, and then he went on board.

A fresh easterly wind had risen. The gulls in the harbour screeched and cried, sailing in broad circles to and fro over the water, gleaming white, arrowing down to the surface like daylight meteors and rising again with some shiny writhing thing in their beaks. Steam whistles cut through the air, boats and barges of all sorts crossed one another's paths, and the sun glowed like a dull-red copper disk through the clouds of chimney smoke. Tomas stood captivated, his eyes following a brilliant white seagull that had just swept so close by his head that he could feel the breath of its broad wings and see its wild-bird soul gleaming forth in its tiny pitch-black eye. It arced a slow semicircle over Skeppsbron, hovered a few seconds above the poplars and the maples in that quiet little secret garden between the wings of the Palace, then headed out east, over the harbour, and was lost in the blue.

The steamboat put out. The narrow alleys round Skeppsbron filed past like a row of dark cellar windows, and on the net of bridges and viaducts that connects the Old Town and the southern district, people were crawling around one another like ants. The wharf of Stadsgården was black with coalers leaving sparkling red wakes and with dockers from whose faces Tomas fancied he saw heavy oaths tumbling out, cursing the heat. The high granite cliff face with its stairway hewn from the rock brought dimly to mind an occasion when, as a schoolboy, he'd walked up those steps in the company of Marta and Greta — it was the Christmas holidays, snow and grey skies . . . That was before he'd realised Marta Brehm was beautiful, and in those days perhaps she was not. Both girls had teased him all the time about something he could no longer remember . . . On the southern hills a small-town idyll took hold, with its cottages and wooden fences and cool dark patches of green. In a hammock beneath a big chestnut tree a girl dressed in red lay sleeping.

The houses of Djurgården danced by, and they passed Blockhusudden. The old dilapidated customs house with its steep tiled roof basked in the sunshine, and in the courtyard, where the grass grew high between the cobblestones, a lazy yellow dog was splayed out, flat as if painted on the ground, all four legs stretched as far as they would go.

Out on Värtan the wind freshened up. The spray swirled around the bow and splashed all the way up to Tomas's face as he stood on the bridge talking to the captain.

As four o'clock approached he went down to the mess deck to eat lunch.

It was almost empty there. Two red-faced country folk had just finished eating as Tomas came in; they paid and went up on deck. At one table sat the steersman, eating with almost religious earnestness. He was heavily suntanned, with dark eyes and a black goatee. A fair young girl waited on him with a servant's complaisant movements, without saying a word.

Tomas drank two glasses of schnapps and a bottle of beer. A true spirit of adventure had now overtaken him and he felt himself out on a voyage of discovery, in search of unknown worlds. He knew nothing about Far Isle. Could people be living there? A few poor fishermen, most likely, god fearing, as fishermen always are, who steal and murder a little when the occasion arises and live on pickled herring . . . Then he recalled hearing talk of mining on Far Isle. Would there be mines and quarries there? Probably they'd been abandoned long ago.

The steersman carried on a hushed conversation with the waitress off at the other end of the room. He pressed her hand and the conversation ended; the girl blushed slightly, and the man went up on deck.

Tomas ordered coffee and chartreuse. The waters had got a little rough out on Baggen Sound. The boat rocked gently on a diagonal, both from port to starboard and from bow to stern, and the waves lapped against the sides of the mess deck. When Tomas turned and looked out through the little circular porthole, the sound seemed like a snow-covered field. The porthole lay so close to the surface of the water that almost nothing could be seen but the white spray from the wave crests: hordes of white sparks, flaring and dying, forever commanding the field of view with their phosphor-like glow.

The sun was already succumbing to the red-edged clouds on the western horizon when the boat put in at the quayside on Far Isle. Tomas had secured the captain's permission to stay overnight in a cabin astern. He stepped ashore and walked slowly up the track, weary and dispirited in advance. A steep and stony path, a white house up on the crown of the hill, a few red cottages, smoke rising from their chimneys in the still air of evening, plumb straight as from Abel's offering to God . . . Why had he come here? What had the sea to do with him? He wasn't even sure you could see the sea from here.

Once he'd reached the hilltop he paused and looked back. The waters of the cove spread shiny as glass before him, broad, silent, cold. The sun had just set, infusing red-violet into the mists over the narrow strip of land furthest to the west. Two or three fishing boats headed slowly landwards, sails slack, oars beating evenly, their splashes ticking time away with the same weary regularity as a clock. The day's scattered clouds had drifted off and gathered themselves in an unmoving mass on the horizon; up above arched an empty blue dome, colder and emptier with every minute that passed.

Tomas stood as if frozen, gazing at the scene. Finally, with a shudder, he turned away and carried on along the road inland. Suddenly he realised from the sound of his footsteps that he must be walking over a bridge. He looked up and observed railings on either side of the way. When he leaned over, his gaze drowned in an abyss that went so deep, into such darkness, that it was impossible to glimpse its end: there was only a greenish dampness, like the glint of sin from a dark eye. This, then, was the mine . . . Tomas tore himself violently away, afraid of engrossing himself in this dark, green glint, and carried on into the woods, where the track narrowed to a steeply sloping path.

Around him the woods were silent; but from far away, from far below, there came a regular deep groaning, the sighings of a giant twisting and turning in his sleep. Tomas stopped and listened. In between the thinning tree trunks he could make out a dead straight edge, dividing the darkening eastern reaches of the sky from something darker and bluer still: the sea.

This was the sea: deep blue, endless, empty.

Down on the shore, Tomas drifted back and forth, his collar turned up, his hands in his pockets. The twilight had ripened to a bluish gloom. The sea slept, but it worked on in its sleep, heaving and falling, sighing and groaning like that giant dreaming malevolent dreams.

He'd reached a rocky outcrop, narrow, steep sided, jutting far out from land: there was the sea, all around, wherever he cast his eyes; the sea was everywhere.

Tomas himself had no idea how long he stood there, still as a statue, staring out over the water.

"Marta!" he muttered to himself, "Marta, Marta . . ."

The sea drowned his voice. He felt his lips moving but heard nothing.

"Marta!" he yelled at last, bellowing with all his might.

And astonished, terrified at the sound of his own frail, hollow voice, thin as a knife blade cutting through the roar of the swell, he turned, his whole body shaking, and, with eyes peeled for assassins hidden behind every bush and thicket, he sought out the path and went running back to the cove on the other side of the island where the boat was moored.

He didn't go on board at once, sensing he would be unable to sleep. He sat on a rock and let his gaze drift, now out over the straits and sounds, now down at the steamboat, a strange little toy human contrivance that lay sandwiched down there between the rocks, reflected in the dark, crystal-green water. Two figures were moving about on deck, sharply defined against the yellow-red evening sky. A thickset man — two dark eyes, a black beard — and the graceful figure of a servant girl, fair of face. She was the one who spoke, and he listened with restless impatience, shifting his weight from one foot to the other, thrusting his hands in his pockets and taking them out again. What was she talking about? Her voice sounded importunate to the point of tears, yet controlled — as if she were reminding him of a promise . . . an old promise, which perhaps he would rather have forgotten . . . And he turned his head away and mumbled something, while her eyes lay fixedly on his lips . . . Then they went in, and silence fell.

It was now eleven o'clock. Tomas boarded the boat, went down into the cabin at the stern and put himself to bed, half undressed, on a couch. For a long time he lay awake, because he was thinking of Marta. Long into the night he fell asleep at last, with the pillow pressed tight to his chest.

VIII

It was drizzling incessantly and the streets smelled of wet tarmac and the bells were ringing out for morning service, because it was Sunday. Tomas came out of a barber's shop, pale and with bloodshot eyes; he'd not been sleeping well these past few weeks.

He'd arranged to meet his mother at St Jacob's Church. Such was the emptiness he had found within and around him that he readily yielded to every passing impulse, and when his mother came into his room in the morning, while he was still in bed, and asked him in her tenderest voice to come to church with her, he hadn't the heart to say no. Of course, he practically never went to church; but perhaps that was not right. Perhaps today was the day his life would change . . .

Such were his thoughts as he walked slowly down Grev Turegatan. He carried no hymnbook in his hand, since he was afraid of running into an acquaintance.

An old lady wearing a threadbare brown coat came out of a doorway, accompanied by a lad wearing his school cap. Both walked at the same tranquil Sunday-morning pace, and each had a hymnbook in hand. Tomas recognised the old woman at once: it was Ellen's mother. He'd seen them together in Humlegården one Sunday afternoon in May. The boy, then, would be Ellen's brother, the one who so wanted to be a doctor . . .

And this was where they lived.

Tomas had stopped outside the doorway. Ellen had in fact once told him that she lived on Grev Turegatan, but obviously he hadn't been able to call on her there.

So if Ellen's at home, she's alone, he thought. *But why isn't she*

76

going to church with her mother and brother — is she ill?

Poor Ellen. His conduct towards her had been beyond the pale — so much so that he hardly dared think about it.

What could she think of him?

Perhaps she was already dead. In three weeks he'd not seen her. She might perfectly well be dead without his knowing anything about it.

Life is strange.

He had to see her, had to know she was alive. Talk to her, explain himself one way or another, fall at her feet and beg forgiveness . . .

He was already on his way up the stairs; they were narrow and steep, and it was so dark on the landings that he had to light one match after another to read the names on the doors. On one peeling and grubby door, which looked as if it ought to lead to a kitchen, he was much surprised to see his match illuminating a name known to him from books and newspapers, whose possessor he had seen on the streets and in bars and cafés many times, always looking cheerful and elegant. Tomas had imagined he must live on Sturegatan or Strandvägen . . .

It was only on the second floor that he found what he was looking for.

He stood awhile hesitating, heart pounding, breath bated, before he could steel himself to pull on the little black and red bell string.

He didn't know what he was going to say to her. Would she believe him, if he said he'd been ill, or had been away for a few weeks? No, she might have spotted him walking past the shop . . .

Besides, he ought actually to break with her; that was why he'd come here. He didn't love her. But whatever he did he should do it fast: in fifteen or at most twenty minutes he had to be at the church, as he'd promised.

Trusting in his impulse he gently pulled on the string.

Nobody answered. He pulled again, harder. He could hear footsteps inside, and now Ellen stood before him. She was wearing a large white apron with a high breast piece, looking like a chaste young matron interrupted in the midst of her chores.

Tomas was lost for words; he stood there red with shame. It was as if he'd never before seen how beautiful she was, although at the moment she was very pale.

Ellen stared at him for a long time with a steely gaze.

"Come in," she said at last, softly, with a little tremor in her voice.

The flat consisted of two small, bright rooms and a kitchen. They were standing in the middle of the outer room, and neither said a word.

"Why didn't you go to church with your mother and brother?" Tomas finally asked quietly, with audible uncertainty.

"I've such a terrible headache," she complained softly. He put his hand on her forehead. It was burning.

Ellen burst into tears.

"Oh Tomas, where have you been all this time?"

He had no answer.

She drew him over to the couch, her hands toying with his hair, sobbing constantly, her head against his chest.

"Where have you been, Tomas? You have to tell me where you've been . . . You must have been ill — tell me you've been ill!"

"Yes," replied Tomas, "I've been ill."

They both sat in silence. The church bells rang outside and the rain spotted against the window sill.

"If only I could believe you," whispered Ellen.

Tomas made no reply.

How was he going to do this? He had to break with her . . .

What to say?

"If only I could believe you," she took up again. "I so want to, but I can't. You don't seem to care very much for me!"

Tomas was anxious. His mother might be waiting for him already. But Ellen's big russet eyes looked into his with such desperation that the courage to say anything decisive failed him.

He just stroked her forehead, as if to cool it.

"Does your head still ache?" he asked.

"Yes, yes . . . Put your hand there — just there — to the left, by the temple . . . that feels so nice!"

She closed her eyes and leant her cheek against his. It burned like a flame. Tomas felt a sweet warmth rushing through the whole of his being. It had been a long time since he'd felt the touch of a woman's skin against his own.

Suddenly he bent forward over her face and kissed her passionately.

She writhed out of his arms and sprang up.

"No, Tomas, you're not to kiss me any more! It's best it's over between us. I'm nothing to you now — there's someone else you like, isn't there? There is! I see it in you, Tomas! You haven't been ill at all — it isn't true!"

She stared at him, a seer's glint in her eyes.

"I knew all along you were lying to me, I've seen you lots of times, walking past the window — lots of times!"

And she sank down on the couch with her head in her hands and cried.

Tomas wanted the earth to swallow him up.

"Forgive me," he stammered.

Now, a canary that all the time had been sitting on its perch in a cage by the window began to twitter: softly at first, as if seeking permission, then ever louder and more piercingly.

"Forgive me," Tomas repeated, pleadingly, "Forgive me! I've been horrible to you, Ellen, dear Ellen, but I will never do it again! You have to look me in the face and tell me you forgive me and that you're not angry with me any more!"

The canary jumped from perch to perch in its cage, held its head aloft and twittered and sang.

"You just don't know what these days have been like for me," Ellen sobbed, "standing behind that counter morning till night, trying on gloves with ladies — strangers, pretty girls, girls you might know, girls you might be with . . . Or looking out of the window and seeing you walk past. I've been lying awake crying all these nights, Tomas —"

Tomas got out his handkerchief, moistened it in water and pressed it against her eyes, and finally kissed her eyelids.

"You're not to cry any more," he said.

She sat in silence on her side of the couch, a cushion beneath her head, and looked him straight in the eye.

"Can I believe you, Tomas?" she said. "Do you really care about me?"

"There's nobody I care about but you," said Tomas.

The canary now began to sing with all its might. It was painful to listen to; you could hardly hear yourself speak. Ellen hurriedly got up and found a dark cloth in a wardrobe; she spread it carefully over the cage, tucking every corner so that no light could get in.

The bird fell silent at once.

Tomas had taken a large, darkly speckled shell from the chest of drawers by the couch, weighed it in his hand and held it up to his ear. His hearing was filled with a muffled, unceasing roar that seemed to emanate either deep within or far away, and which brought to mind the sea . . . and a name that once he had stood calling out into the sea. A name he could not forget.

Ellen sat by his side again, and her gaze came to rest on his.

"If you're fond of me, say it three times," she said, shy and embarrassed, a tear in her eyelashes still.

Tomas said it three times.

But he found it hard to look her in the eye. His gaze drifted from the colourful stripes on the mat beneath his feet, to the floral pattern on the upholstery, to the white, home-sewn blanket on the bed.

"You know," said Ellen reflectively, "when once you've taken the wrong path it's hard to turn back. That's why you mustn't leave me, Tomas; you have to help me . . . I don't *want* to become a bad girl!"

The bells had stopped ringing, and water splashed constantly from the guttering. The rain poured down more heavily and the skies had darkened. Now and then the canary gave out a little peep from under his brown cloak, till at last he quietened completely and fell asleep; he thought it was night.

Tomas and Ellen sat silently. His arm had crept round her waist. He felt her starting to yield, and a dreamy look rose in her eyes.

IX

Tomas Weber was so bored he devoted himself to his studies for days on end. The relationship with Ellen was not as before. He was weary; she still mistrusted him, but spared herself no humiliation to hold onto him. Every new elation was followed by an awakening when they stared wordlessly at one another, like two strangers, he in boredom, she dreading the coldness in his eyes; for he had changed, drifted from her. He had become someone other than the Tomas who chanced across her path one bright spring morning, whom she had loved, thoughtlessly and young, and before whose passion she had not withheld one ounce of her being.

Yet there had been no scenes full of reproaches and mutual recrimination; they simply sensed the gulf between them widening more each day, and how futile were their attempts to bridge it.

Thus the days passed, colourless and empty, and the days into weeks, without his counting them.

It was the end of July already.

*

Tomas met up with Karl Hammer at the Victoria, the cool, shady little summer bar in Kungsträdgården. Hammer had just returned from a short stay at Consul Arvidson's country home by Lake Mälaren; he'd had a few weeks free from his official duties.

The summer sun had worked in vain on his colourless complexion. He sat there, white-faced as a painted clown,

sipping his vermouth with the same expression of pale for-
bearance as ever.

They talked about women.

Wenschen and Grenholm, the factory owner, sat at a table
nearby drinking cognac and water; after a while Dr Rehn
appeared and joined them.

All three gentlemen's wives were staying in the country.

Grenholm had the head of a Roman patrician, now sprouting grey, set on a rather substantial body. Dr Rehn was an
imposing and still-slender gentleman of about fifty.

They were talking politics. Wenschen was a freethinker,
without being in the least radical, but he was constantly being
shouted down by Grenholm and Rehn, who held identical
opinions — staunchly conservative ones.

Gabriel Mortimer came strolling past the café. When he
saw Tomas and Hammer he dropped in to say hello and invite
Tomas over to Dalarö the following Sunday with his mother.
He was on his way to catch a boat, but was in no hurry and sat
down to drink a bottle of mineral water.

Discussion had turned to the latest literature, among other
things to a certain novelist whose name had come to promi-
nence a few years before in the different literary climate then
prevailing, itself a consequence of a reaction against the nation's foremost writer. He was one of many of those '1880s'
men' who'd subsequently had second thoughts. Hammer was
just sitting there talking about one of his books when the man
himself walked past in the avenue outside.

The three men smiled.

Karl Hammer's smile was withering.

"What fellow feeling such a man must have with that old
ass Peter, who lasted all the way to the third crowing of the
cock before betraying his master," he said.

Gabriel Mortimer's smile was blithely indulgent.

"He'd probably rather have been the cockerel."

Tomas Weber didn't so much smile as laugh out loud, but it was just the laughter of a child over something the adults tell him is ridiculous. Besides, he really did think the writer looked comical, striding away sweating in the heat and all the time striving to maintain his proper writer's bearing.

Mortimer had just noticed the same thing.

"When it's twenty degrees in the shade everyone looks like a travelling salesman," he said.

Wenschen looked at his watch, rose, bid his company farewell and left. Tomas, Mortimer and Hammer exchanged a friendly greeting with him as he passed their table. Wenschen did not look happy; in point of fact he had domestic troubles of his own. Mrs Wenschen had not excited attention for two years, but now everybody knew that she had a new lover: Grothusen.

Tomas sat wondering when he'd next manage to see Johannes Hall. He needed to borrow some money from him. That morning he'd got a postcard from Hall, postmarked Wiesbaden; Jean Arvidson spent his summers down there and Hall had gone with him and been keeping him company for a few weeks. His plan now was to take a tour of some German towns he'd wanted to visit or revisit, after which he'd perhaps settle in some spa town on the coast of Själland for the remainder of the summer.

Mortimer got up and took his leave; he had to catch his boat. Once more he asked Tomas over to Dalarö next Sunday with his mother, and Tomas promised to come.

Grenholm and Dr Rehn were involved in a quiet, confidential conversation. Grenholm seemed perturbed for some reason or other; his eyes seemed slightly misted, and several times he patted his friend on the arm. But then the very moment one of the waitresses came near he started patting her instead, on the tummy, and asking for the bill.

Tomas and Hammer were more or less alone in the place

now.

Insects buzzed around them. A soothing coolness prevailed in the deep shadow that drowsed beneath the foliage and the black network of branches of the old lindens, and grew deeper still tight by the buildings' dark, grey walls.

Old beggar women, flower girls and invalids with nickel rings came in one after another wanting to do business. Tomas, who was easily moved to pity and had hitherto seen little of the hardships of the world, opened up his wallet time and again while Hammer looked on, impassive as a stone, smiling coldly at his liberality.

"Do you ever write anything nowadays?" asked Tomas, when at last the silence grew too long.

Hammer was in no hurry to answer, as if he found the question somewhat uncalled for.

"Oh yes," he said drily, "I write this and that occasionally. When I've time and inclination. But I don't publish."

"Why not?"

"I've plenty of patience. I'm biding my time. It'll come."

They had nothing more to say to each other; and besides Tomas was headed home to eat, it was past four already; he paid for his vermouth and left. On the way out he got a nod from one of the waitresses, a lively girl with dark eyes with whom he'd been on good terms the summer before. He returned it with a scampish grin.

Hammer was left sitting alone.

On the way home Tomas contemplated his finances. Where could he get money? He had only a few öre left in his wallet; that wasn't even enough for an after-dinner cigar. Father would be back from Germany in a week; he'd have to talk to him then. It would be disagreeable but it couldn't be put off any longer.

But how could he go about getting a cigar? Not having a

cigar to smoke with coffee after dinner: that was pretty much like having toothache.

He was just passing a cigar shop where he was a very good customer. Might he drop in as usual, ask for a cigar, and then pretend he'd left his wallet at home . . . in the pocket of another coat?

After a moment's hesitation he went in, but he stopped in his tracks with alarm when behind the counter he saw an old woman instead of the young girl who normally stood there.

"Sorry, wrong shop," he muttered, furious, and turned round abruptly and vanished.

No cigar today, then; salvation was nowhere to be found!

This misfortune put him in a black mood. Involuntarily he came to think of those unhappy schooldays when during break he'd been thrashed by some stronger classmate, only to get a black mark from the teacher for inattentiveness during the next lesson; and then, when the bell brought the school day to an end, he'd come running home, angry and hungry, and find dried cod waiting for him for supper.

He could almost swear it would be dried cod this evening too, never mind that he couldn't recall their ever having had it since he was a child.

On Biblioteksgatan he spotted Anton Recke. At once he went over to him to cadge fifty öre for a cigar: he'd left his wallet at home.

"Come off it," laughed Recke. "Nobody leaves his wallet at home if it's still got something in it."

Tomas made no attempt to maintain his assertion.

Recke took a couple of cigars from his case and stuffed them in Tomas's breast pocket. Then the two went a little way up towards Östermalm together.

"By the way," said Recke as they parted, "you're perfectly welcome to borrow a tenner if you like."

Tomas thanked him and promised to pay it back as soon

as he could. Recke smiled sceptically.

"I'm rich for the time being," he added. "I've been to see the brick merchant at Svartmangatan."

It wasn't dried cod for supper; it was veal cutlet with cauliflower.

"By the way, a letter came for you," said his mother as they rose from the table. "It's in your room."

Tomas stood by his desk. He was holding the letter in his hand, staring at it, pale with emotion.

He couldn't believe his eyes.

It was the same beloved, disguised handwriting on the envelope he knew so well from all those little notes he'd been reading and rereading since the beginning of summer.

What could she have to say to him? Were there new miseries, some new misfortune lying hidden, awaiting him in this innocent little white envelope?

He tore it open and read.

Tomas — Meet me on Döbelnsgatan tomorrow at half past five. I have something to tell you.

That was all. The note was dated yesterday.

It had just got to twenty past five. He took his hat and his cane and ran down the stairs.

What did she want to tell him?

He took the shortest route, down through Humlegården.

By Linnaeus' statue he raised his hat to Pastor Caldén, pacing to and fro amongst the clumps of flowers, deep in meditation, his cold, severe features seeming more benevolent and as it were softened in the tranquillity of the afternoon sun.

He'd been Tomas's religious instructor at school; when he saw Tomas passing and greeting him he took him kindly by the hand and started to ask him about his studies and his plans for the future. After a few memorable words about the medical profession he drew Tomas over to the nearest clump of flowers and for the next few minutes stood there thoughtfully without saying a word.

Tomas was on tenterhooks. Marta might be waiting already . . . what was coming, something about God's immanence?

Still Pastor Caldén stood lost in silent contemplation.

"It's beautiful, this," he said at last in a subdued, introverted tone.

"Yes," said Tomas.

"But I don't like the colours. I can't abide all this red. Look, wherever you turn — red everywhere, just red. You can stare yourself blind on it."

And he added quietly, as if in thought, "No: white flowers and white souls . . ."

Tomas stood there squirming. Finally the pastor noticed and his face quickly resumed its familiar expression.

"I see you're in a hurry," he said smiling. "Well, take care now, and give my regards to your father."

And he walked slowly off and sat down to dream on one of the benches, amid the gentle sunlight.

Tomas set off through one of the alleys leading down to Roslagstorg. He was still somewhat amazed: Pastor Caldén never used to be sentimental . . .

On the wooden steps up to St Johannes' churchyard the black cat with the white front paws was still sitting on its threshold sunning itself. Tomas allowed himself a moment to stop and stroke the cat's back.

Marta was standing in the doorway of the apartment block on Döbelnsgatan. She was very pale, her eyes so wide.

"Have you been waiting?" asked Tomas in a veiled half-voice as he fumbled for her hand. At last she offered it to him and let him press it.

"No, I just got here," she said, without meeting his gaze.

And she ushered him up the stairs ahead of her without another word. Words failed Tomas too. What was this all about? What did she have to say to him?

He saw how her hand was trembling as she put the key in the lock.

They stood in the middle of the drawing room, staring at one another in silence. All was as it had been: the same heavy air, the same mysterious yellow light. Through an open window came the sound of footsteps tramping on the pavement outside.

Finally Marta began to speak.

"So, well, you see, Tomas . . . I can't live without you; it's not possible; it can't be done . . . and the whole thing was my fault . . . let it all turn out as it will . . ."

She could say nothing more, her voice failed her. And two big tears shone in her eyes as she grasped his head between her trembling hands and showered him with a summer storm of kisses.

X

Now September.

Tomas was no longer living at home; no one but he and Marta knew why. He did still eat at his parents', however, since otherwise he would not have eaten at all. He'd rented a low-ceilinged attic room in a decrepit old house up by Adolf Fredrik Church, a shabby little room with a sloping floor and old-fashioned furniture, whose only window overlooked a paved yard with big rustling trees. There in the mornings he would lie on the couch with a book in his hand, though he didn't read much; mainly he brooded over how he might earn money — at any rate until, on fine days, the sun angled in through the window pane, began its play among the wallpaper's withered flowers, cut short his broodings and tempted him out. There too Tomas and Marta spent most of the slowly fading afternoons of late summer, arms wrapped round each other, and the seconds rushed by and became minutes and the minutes sped away in hurried flight, like sand before the wind, while they, eyes shut, listened to the whisperings in the branches of the elms, till both together held their breath and suddenly their eyes stood open, staring into each other with secret wonder, each reading in the other's eyes the same silent question, borne on the wind and accompanied by the wind's song outside: *Where will it all lead? Where will it all lead?*

*

Tomas came walking down Sturegatan. He could spend whole mornings drifting around the streets steered by nothing but the whims of the moment, while new layers of dust were deposited over the textbooks on the shelves at home. He was happy, but not at ease. He was walking with the wind behind him, and downhill, and breathing easy: but he didn't know where he was going.

When he reached Stureplan he went into a flower shop to buy flowers for Marta; he would often do this when he had money. The night before he'd packed up a pile of old novels and poetry collections in a box and gone out in the wind and rain to sell them to a second-hand book dealer. It wasn't until he was standing there at the counter and the near-sighted old book dealer was warily inspecting the offerings, one by one — it wasn't until then that he noticed he'd packed up *Heritage and Youth* by Jacob Ahrenberg. His first thought had been to set it aside and keep it, but when the dealer leafed through it with obvious interest and offered a particularly high price, he let it go with all the rest.

He chose a little bouquet of white Malmaison roses, paid and asked for them to be delivered that afternoon.

He specified his own address.

When he came out Greta was standing waiting for him. She'd been walking along and stopped by the window to have a look at the new orchids; among others, she'd inspected one that was very much like the orchid Johannes Hall had in his buttonhole at the Arvidsons'. Then she'd chanced to look deeper into the shop, and there was Tomas buying white roses.

Probing interrogation began at once.

"*Who* are you buying flowers for?" she asked indignantly. "You have to tell me."

Tomas maintained an enigmatic silence.

"They're for an elderly lady," he said at last. "An elderly lady whose sixtieth birthday it is today, and to whom I must send a token of my regard," he added solemnly, indicating that he would, if possible, prefer to be believed.

"Oh you fibber! You don't know any old lady that I don't know."

Standing there in the middle of the street Greta pinched his arm so hard it really hurt.

The summer down in Scania had tanned her red and brown, and her small bosom had acquired a softer, more pronounced rounding.

"You're just jealous because you're not getting any flowers yourself," said Tomas.

And he drew her into the shop, bought a big red rose and tucked it in by her breast.

She flushed with delight, but her inquisitiveness only grew.

"You seem to be rolling in it," she said as they came out onto the street. "Where in the world is it all coming from?"

"I robbed a bank," said Tomas seriously.

Greta eyed him with alarm. In point of fact she found this story more plausible than the one about the old lady.

They walked along Birger Jarlsgatan together; Greta was on her way to a friend who lived out on Strandvägen. She was rid of school at last and enjoying her new-found freedom to the full.

For a long time she was quiet, as if thinking about something she didn't really dare come out with.

At the junction with Hamngatan they parted.

"You know what, Tomas?" she said at last, taking her leave. "I know perfectly well why it is you don't want to live at home!"

Greta had blushed bright red, but she was looking him straight in the eye.

Tomas found it hard to hide his unease.

"Well?"

"Mum thinks it's so you can come home as late as you want without her knowing, and dad thinks it's so you can drink with your mates and sit up all night playing cards. But that's not what I think. I think it's because you've found some tart you want to be with!"

What she was saying so embarrassed her that there were tears in her voice by the end.

Tomas was relieved.

"No, Greta, you misjudge me," he replied, as gravely as he could.

She looked sceptically at him; then they went their separate ways.

Tomas walked through Berzelii Park. Shadows lay quiet and deep beneath the trees' still fresh, bluishly dark-green canopies. Suddenly he stopped. Wasn't that Ellen over there, coming towards him? Indeed it was Ellen! It was too late to turn round, and there were no other paths nearby he could divert into. What to say to her? He'd not seen her in over a month. Since then he'd written to her breaking it off.

His eyes burrowed into the ground and he walked straight ahead. When next he looked up she was gone.

He turned off into the narrow winding alleyway by the synagogue and reached Kungsträdgården. It was just past noon. The sandy pathways through the broad avenues of trees, still empty from the summer season, shone chalk-white in the stark midday sun, thinly shaded by the small round sooty canopies of the young trees. Outside the Royal Theatre a couple of actors stood yawning, hats in front of their faces.

Tomas went down along Blasieholmen quay. On coming past the Grand Hôtel he went into the Oriental for a vermouth.

It was much busier than it used to be. The gloomy waiters, whose pale shadows had once slid back and forth along the walls in the deathly silence of the corridors, had vanished and been replaced by odalisques in parti-coloured silk rags. Along with them came the clientele, smoking and drinking everywhere. In one of the alcoves, where a red gas flame fluttered constantly in the half-light, there sat Lieutenant Gabel with a half-dozen other young officers, a few of them in uniform. They were discussing the question of the Union of Crowns.

Tomas took a seat by an open window, the same place he'd sat with Hall on one of those late April days just after his examination success.

Yes — where had Hall got to? He'd stayed at that Danish spa for three weeks; then he'd started up on his travels again, wandering aimlessly. Perhaps the sheer duration of it was its own satisfaction . . . When he last wrote he was in Germany.

Now, though, he'd have to be back sharpish, otherwise Tomas would have to inquire at that brick merchant's.

Well, he could do that anytime regardless — the sooner the better. Maybe today. He had in mind going and asking about terms and conditions; there was no danger in that by itself. It was true that Wannberg, who had connections with a couple of publishers, had promised to try to get him some translation work, but that could take time. He thought of that income rather as something more long-term, when it came to settling the most important of his debts.

Sitting there Tomas had subsided a little. His head had sunk between his shoulders without his noticing.

He was tired: not so much physically, but his inner being had been enfeebled by the ceaseless gyration between the rosiest of joys and the grey qualms of reflection. One moment he saw himself holding beaming happiness itself in his arms, the next his hands were groping in the empty air.

He straightened up, emptied his glass and poured another. In the alcove the officers had moved on to a new topic: Mrs Wenschen and Grothusen. Baron Grothusen had wearied, especially as he — so it was said — was preoccupied with more serious matters; thus he'd made an excursion to Paris to put the affair behind him. But a week later Mrs Wenschen had also left town — word being that she'd gone after him.

"Indeed," said Lieutenant Gabel, "it's by no means inexplicable when you come to think of it. Mrs Wenschen has in all probability never experienced true passion before; and she's thirty-six now . . ."

The others agreed, and one — amid the laughter of the others — pitied Mr Wenschen, who was now going round explaining that his wife had gone to visit relatives in Copenhagen.

Tomas looked out of the window, gazing at the passers-by on the pavement. Suddenly his heart skipped a beat: Mrs Brehm and Marta were going past. She noticed him, and her eyes lit up, while all the time looking straight ahead, serious and correct.

She was slender and pale.

Tomas sat for a long time thinking about Marta. He didn't know the reason, but he almost felt as if he wanted to cry. What would the future bring? Would Marta Brehm perhaps one day become a Mrs Wenschen?

The room had quietened; Gabel and his company had gone.

Tomas was still lost in thought. Two fantastical stylised birds on a blue and yellow door ornament regarded him sternly, relentlessly with their empty round eyes.

So, then, the brick merchant.

He got up and left.

He took the launch over to Gustav III's statue and went up Slottsbacken. It took a while before he found Svartmangatan among the spider web of alleyways encircling Stortorget. He slipped in through an entryway and up some stairs, knocked on a door and heard a voice respond: "Come in!"

Tomas felt as if he was about to sit an exam. He steeled himself, opened the door and entered a fairly large room with cornflower-blue wallpaper; the blinds, drawn down against the sun, shone a more vivid blue. A short, plumpish man of about forty in a checked summer suit, propping himself in an ingratiating pose against the office desk, observed him with expectant interest.

Tomas recognised the brick merchant at once from Recke's description. Besides, he had a feeling that he'd seen him once before, but couldn't remember when or under what circumstances. It was the man's lively ginger-brown eyes in particular that seemed familiar.

Tomas gave his name and mentioned his friend, Mr Recke, and explained his business. He was interested in discussing the terms of a small loan — his circumstances were temporarily embarrassed — specifically 300 kronas.

When the brick merchant heard the name Recke he made a complicit gesture towards a yellow-upholstered Windsor chair, while himself remaining in his half-sitting, half-standing posture that recalled at once the autocrat and the broad-minded newspaper editor and the provincial stand-up comic. When Tomas came to the number 300 a look of derision reflexively crossed his face, but in the very next moment he was once more serious, concerned, almost austere.

"Indeed these are hard times — uncertain times. Every day I make losses. You're a medical student, then, sir? In your second year, indeed . . . Yes, well, as I say, I'm making constant losses . . ."

He minced to and fro with his hands behind his back.

Losses . . . Tomas had the peculiarly unnerving sensation of having experienced this scene before. He was utterly convinced that one time or another he'd heard this same plaintive voice talking about this or that loss, his eyes darting hither and thither.

"And of course in any case, sir, I'm not properly acquainted with your circumstances . . ."

Tomas squirmed in his seat. What should he say? He stared at the colourful cover of an American detective novel lying closed on the desk, a strip of newspaper serving as a bookmark. Should he perhaps just get up and go, sooner now than later?

"What was it now, 300 kronas?" the brick merchant began again. "Of course the sum is of lesser concern. Indeed, with a reputable guarantor it could be that much and twenty times as much as well. But without — nothing."

Guarantor? To Tomas this made no sense at all. With a reputable guarantor you could borrow freely at a bank or anywhere else, and at a good rate too. Why would anyone turn to a brick merchant if he had a guarantor?

"Indeed," he responded with sangfroid, "and I hope the guarantors I propose will be acceptable to you."

The brick merchant looked at him with surprise.

"I hope so too," he said with a warm, hearty tone that struck Tomas as so old and familiar he almost felt afraid.

"Now, sir, the terms you were inquiring after. With such a small sum, and a completely unfamiliar client, I couldn't contemplate a term in excess of three months. Let us then draw up the guarantee for 375 kronas, an interest rate of six per cent."

He was still pacing the room with hands behind his back. Suddenly he stopped right in front of Tomas, resuming his initial posture — back against the desk, one leg crossed over the other.

"Are you of full age, sir?" he asked abruptly.

Tomas was quite taken aback. But he rose, unperturbed, and began flicking with one glove.

"Full age? Yes of course I am," he replied in that indifferently distracted tone he had, of late, learned to adopt whenever a lie was called for.

So now you had to be of full age, too, to borrow money off a brick merchant, as well as having a guarantor, and the devil and his mother . . .

"Well then, let's say we meet here again at the same time

on Wednesday, with the papers signed."

He accompanied Tomas to the door.

"Weber," he murmured to himself, "Weber . . . You wouldn't by any chance be Professor Weber's son, sir?"

"Yes," replied Tomas curtly.

"Ah, indeed . . . Hm. Well, there's every prospect we shall be able to do business . . . Till Wednesday, then."

And, poking his head round the door, he added, "Do watch out for the stairs; there's a piece missing from one of the topmost steps. The landlord here has little concern for the welfare of his fellow man!"

Tomas made his way home via the Palace. He was lost in thought, seeing nothing left or right. So he had to get a couple of guarantors, one way or another.

Where will it all lead?

When he reached the outer courtyard he stopped and slapped his hand to his brow: now he knew where he'd seen the brick merchant before. One spring day many years ago, when he was still a schoolboy, he'd gone out to Haga Park with three classmates to collect plants for their studies. On the way they'd passed through the Northern Cemetery and stopped to look at a funeral. There was a humble coffin, accompanied by a few simple folk. Apart from the priest there was only one person in the whole procession whose dress suggested an affiliation with the better classes, a plumpish little man with lively ginger-brown eyes. The coffin was lowered into the ground and the priest conducted the ceremonies as fast as he could. Then the little man stepped up onto the mound of earth and started to speak; and the onlookers respectfully bared their heads while he, emotion in his voice and eyes turned heavenwards, expounded on those left behind, and on their loss.

XI

It was one of the glorious days of autumn.

The thinning trees of Humlegården shone red and yellow. Like enormous migrating birds whose broad dark wings could hide the sun for minutes at a time and plunge the earth into shadow, ragged shreds of cloud glided hastily, restlessly across an October sky so vividly blue it seemed to belong to a warmer, more southerly autumn. A storm had blown up overnight. Paths and lawns were strewn with snapped twigs and fallen leaves and whole branches had been broken off, and still the wind was singing in the canopies, while down below gusts twirled one madly dancing pillar of earth and sand and mottled leaves after another.

Tomas and Marta had arranged to meet in the northern part of the park, by the elder tree beneath which, one warm day in June, she'd woken him by tickling his lips with a blade of grass.

"It's a wonderful day," said Tomas. "We must find something to do!"

"Yes," said Marta, quietly and hesitant, "We must find something . . ."

And she gazed silently upon him, eyes wide open. Finally she looked hurriedly around, pressed herself tight to him and kissed him. There was nobody near but an old Daleswoman who was walking stooped and crooked across the lawn, raking up leaves.

Then she burst into tears.

"What's got into you?" asked Tomas.

His voice was agitated.

"Nothing, nothing . . ."

She dried her tears, and after a few minutes she was back to her usual self, bright and cheery. They went together down towards the centre of town, unbothered by the people teeming all around them.

The streets were lively today.

On Biblioteksgatan Tomas was nearly run over from behind by a cab. In the cab sat Consul Arvidson and Jean. The cabbie quietened the horses for a moment and passing greetings were exchanged. The consul radiated youth and health and his handshake was soft and warm. Jean was pale as usual, and his gaze drifted off along the rows of buildings as he extended Tomas his cold and clammy hand.

"He doesn't look well," said Marta.

"No . . ."

A hidden unease had come over Tomas the moment he shook Consul Arvidson's hand. Why had he hit upon the idea of using his signature — his and Gabriel Mortimer's — on the brick merchant's contract? It would have been better if he'd used someone else's — someone he didn't know and had never met — anyone at all, in other words. The brick merchant knew perfectly well it was a forgery in any case. Tomas had seen it in the smile on his face when he took the document and handed over the money. That smile was simply shameless. Oh well, it was of no account: he was bound be able to get hold of some money in three months, and nobody would be any the wiser. Nobody in the whole world would be any the wiser — and he meant to forget it too once the whole thing was over and the papers torn up, burned, gone. Who'd remember it then, when he'd forgotten it himself?

They'd come out into Kungsträdgårdsgatan.

Lieutenant Gabel was walking just ahead of them; smoke from his cigar hit them in the face, and Marta couldn't help but sneeze. He was wearing perfectly ordinary dark, striped trousers: thanks to Mrs Wenschen, the tale of Gabel's trousers had reached such a wide audience that it was no longer possible for him to wear them, or indeed any other ostentatious trousers at all.

Tomas felt the light tap of a hand on his shoulders. It was his father, passing him with hurried steps and a friendly nod of the head, while briskly raising his hat to Marta. He was in a great hurry, on his way to a bank. Professor Weber had latterly been highly satisfied with his son, there having been no talk of money for a long time. He thus assumed that Tomas had started to sort himself out, and was waiting only for him to move back home again, the sooner the better.

"So, what shall we do?" asked Tomas. "There might not be that many fine days left now . . . And you have an engagement this afternoon."

The professor was already well ahead of them when Tomas saw him exchange a brief greeting with a short gentleman wearing a checked summer suit beneath a buttoned overcoat. The brick merchant . . . Did father know him too?

The next moment Lieutenant Gabel also acknowledged him, and then it was Tomas's turn. The brick merchant's smile when he returned the greeting intimated politeness and tact, but he did not take his cigar out of his mouth.

"Who was that?" asked Marta.

"It's one of my old teachers," replied Tomas. "He's an able mathematician, but very absent minded. Otherwise he'd probably take his cigar out of his mouth when he says hello."

The sun burned on the pavements. They crossed the road and came into the avenues, where the lindens' yellow-grey leaves danced around their feet.

Justice Ratsman went by in one of the side avenues; he turned his head away and didn't acknowledge them. Tomas had once harboured a certain inexplicable antipathy towards him, but ever since learning that one day in July Marta had turned him down, he felt almost a kind of friendship. He was also a correct and agreeable man in every respect.

"We're out of luck today," Marta remarked. "We hardly ever go out walking together, and now we're meeting all our acquaintances, one after another. We need to tread paths where no one will see us."

She'd hardly spoken when Gabriel Mortimer came past; he was on the way to his office. He greeted them half confidingly, while regarding them with a look at once smiling and sad from his bulging, near-sighted eyes.

"Why don't we go out to Drottningholm," suggested Tomas. "It should be beautiful there on a day like today. And we needn't be afraid of meeting anyone we know now all the summer guests have moved back home."

"Drottningholm — yes . . . It's beautiful there. In the park, by the swannery."

They'd reached one of the side paths that lead to Molin's fountain. A couple of little street urchins were lying on their front on the stone ledge at its base, splashing the water with their hands; they were arguing about a fish that was supposed to be there, a fish that could do tricks, whose master the grubbiest of the lads claimed to be. Otherwise it was quiet and empty around the fountain. The pale-silver willows, which are the last of the trees in Kungsträdgården to shed their late, slowly yellowing leaves, seemed to be bowing their still-summery crowns down together into a quietly plaintive circle around the eight black bronze swans.

"Yes, let's go out to Drottningholm."

Tomas and Marta stood alone on the deck of the *Tessin*. The strait between Lovön and Kersön was almost calm, shielded from the wind by Kersön's elevated forested shoreline. But the restless surface, here rippled, there still, made a shimmering, fragmented mirror image of the wonderful white

summer palace, whose central part, with its high and grace-
fully curving copper roof, struck a powerful outline against the
blue of the autumn sky, while the green patinas of the wings'
cupolas, like tired heads sunken back against pillows, stood out
against red and yellow foliage. The steps down to the water
shone white in the sun, as if made of marble. An old castle
servant was sitting on the quayside, half asleep, a fishing rod
in his hand, a grey-haired man with livery buttoned up and
brilliantly gleaming buttons on his coat.

Tomas and Marta went up to the inn to eat a late breakfast.
They found a large, low-ceilinged room with flowery curtains
hanging in front of old-style sixteen-paned windows, through
which the view was almost completely obscured by wild red
vines whose encircled and entwined ranks climbed up along
the walls. In the middle of the broad bench where they sat a
large white cat lay asleep.

Tomas carefully closed the door behind the maid who
served them.

"I'm so happy today," said Marta, when, after the meal,
they walked along the avenue of now bare poplars towards the
palace, past the chapel wing and down into the park.

"I feel as if nothing bad could ever happen to us. The
clouds are sailing past us up there; it's not us they're going to
rain on today. They're sailing off to distant lands, and they're
going to burst over people I don't know and don't care about."

Tomas didn't answer at once. He was looking at the
clouds mirrored in the park's watercourses and ponds. In the
dark water they took on a deeper shade than up in the sky.

"But you were crying when we were in Humlegården," he
said at last.

Marta was silent.

"Why did you cry when you kissed me? Tell me why you
were crying!"

"It was nothing . . . I just felt so despondent for a moment;

I don't know why myself. Probably it was nothing anyway."

"You have to tell me what it was!"

"No, not now. Some other time, perhaps, but not today."

They walked slowly down one of the linden avenues, four trees abreast. The narrow strip of sky untouched by the tapering vault of the trees' branches shone above their heads with that emptily bright, frozen shade which colours the blue of the sky when the sun goes behind clouds.

A wagtail ran in front of their feet, back and forth in an aimless zigzag; she had a long worm in her beak.

"Where does that path lead?" asked Marta, pointing to one in among the trees. "Do you suppose it leads to China?"

"Well, let's see . . ."

And they turned off into the pathway. They had not gone far when the trees thinned and the Chinese Pavilion stood before them. The sun was shining just above the turquoise roof and the little towers with their hundreds of bells that had long tired of ringing when the wind stirred them. The angriest autumn storm would not have drawn a sound from their rusty throats, because they no longer had any clappers.

Only for a while did the sun still shine, for the clouds were growing ever thicker. An enormous cotton-white cloud, like a giant hot-air balloon cut loose from its basket and flung pilotless out on some haphazard joyride through the sky, came sailing slowly over from the east, conquering nation after nation on the map of the heavens, and plunging the park into a grey gloom.

Tomas and Marta stood leaning on an old chestnut tree, from whose boughs the wind shook down a rain of yellow leaves over their shoulders. And it was not just the leaves of the chestnut tree that fanned around their heads and stuck in their clothes: the wind drove leaves from all kinds of trees into their arms and at their feet — the reds of the maples, the dark green of the aspens, the brown of the beeches and the yellow-white of the elms. One of the very biggest, a vivid-red maple leaf with dark veins, spent a long time dancing to and fro before their eyes. They both stood watching it.

"Where will it come to rest?"

Suddenly a violent gust sent it straight into Tomas's face. He wanted to pull it away, but Marta leant in and pressed it hard over his eyes with both her hands, kissing his lips all the time. Tomas didn't move. He stood still and let her do with him as she would, while the light shone rose-red in his eyes through the gossamer fabric of the leaf, as the sunlight can sometimes glow red through a child's or a young woman's slender hand. She kissed him a lot, for a long time, but when at last he threw his arms round her neck in passion, to pull her to him and hold her captive, she wriggled out of his embrace lightning fast and took flight down the park.

"Catch me if you can," she cried, "and then do with me as you will!"

Before he could catch her up she'd vanished deep within the network of passageways between the manicured hedges of a winding French maze.

He couldn't find her, and got no answer when he called her name. Having long searched the maze in vain, all its passages and alcoves, he walked dejectedly to the grassy embankment outside and peered in every direction. She might long since have sneaked out of the shrubbery and hidden somewhere else. Where would he find her?

There was no clue as far as the eye could see. The lawns lay quiet and empty with the old baroque yellow sandstone fountain in the middle. And up above the flocks of clouds were chasing one another from east to west in ever greater haste.

Maybe she'd fallen over somewhere and cracked her head against a rock, and was now lying unconscious and bloodied with nobody to help her . . .

"Marta, where are you?"

He went back into the maze and began the search anew.

Suddenly there she was, right in front of him, but she hadn't seen him. She was standing, quiet and erect, looking at a white Venus in a corner of a secluded bosquet. It was a marble Venus, and on her feet and legs, and indeed all the way up to her stomach, vulgar people had scrawled their vulgar names commemorating one boiling hot day or other when some packed steamboat with sprigs fore and aft and an out-of-tune brass band playing on board brought them out here on a pleasure trip to gape and gawp at the remnants of their forefathers' — no, their forefathers' masters' — glory. Her breasts and her proud head gleamed white and impassive; there the barbarians' hands had not reached. At her feet the grass grew lush and soft.

Tomas crept up silently behind Marta, wrapped his arms round her waist, kissed her and forced her down in the grass.

The effigy of Venus stood smiling and white and quiet.

The wind had blown up to a storm. The wild chase of the cloudbanks rushed across the firmament like the dispersing hordes of a defeated army in flight.

Marta was walking in front, her coat flapping in the wind; Tomas followed.

"Where are you going, Marta?"

"There's an old tower on the hill over there — there between the trees — I want to get up high, somewhere with a view . . ."

The trees clacked and the air sang above their heads.

The dark waters of the swannery rippled into small conical lead-grey waves with peaks of seething white foam.

A crash like the sound of a building collapsing brought them to a halt. It was an old, rotten ash tree, completely bare, split by the storm, which had tottered and fallen, and in falling smashed a bridge, one of the miniature hump-backed bridges that cross the channels and with their delicate white balustrades call to mind the toy bridges in a Venetian pantomime. A white swan, swimming around alone in the channel, head held high, dived under the water in alarm and for a long time remained hidden. When he emerged again he swam hurriedly ashore, flew up onto the roof of the swan house and settled there, flapping his wings and emitting strange, strangled cries.

"Let's take a different path," said Tomas.

Marta smiled.

"Trees could blow over on any path," she replied.

But she'd turned pale nonetheless.

The storm made it hard for them to speak. They could hardly breathe as they slowly worked their way up the hill on which the tower stood. The tower was an old dilapidated water tower, whose rust-red wall showed gaping black holes where bricks were missing, either in whole or part. Tomas thumped with the head of his cane on the closed iron door, to which there had surely long been no key. It answered with a boom that for a second drowned out the storm.

The sun shone for a few moments from the sulphur-yellow cleft in a torn cloud.

Below and all around them a heaving sea billowed red and yellow waves, a sea of trees in autumn colours. Beyond the park and the palace Lake Mälaren was seething green and white.

Tomas and Marta stood in the lee of the tower, resting against the wall, listening to the sound of the storm. She leant her head against his chest, and he stared out, not himself knowing what he was thinking.

An old weather vane squeaked up above, and the air sang and withered leaves fluttered round like motley butterflies. Birds nesting in the walls came flying with piercing shrieks.

Tomas suddenly felt this little brown-haired head resting against his chest shake with a stifled sob.

"Why are you crying?" he whispered.

"No, I'm not crying . . ."

"I want to know why you're crying, Marta! Has something bad happened?"

"No, really, it's nothing. Some other time I can tell you, but not now. Come on, Tomas, let's go."

The *Tessin* had already departed when they reached the quay; neither of them had kept track of time. It was after half past two. Nothing remained but to go down to Nockeby bridge and await one of the Svartsjöland boats.

There were only ten minutes to spare.

The sky clouded over ever more. The path curved grey and empty among the groves, abandoned summer villas, fields and marshes. Not a soul was to be seen. It was as if autumn and the dark evenings had laid waste to the land at a single stroke.

The telegraph wires by the wayside droned monotonously.

A little dark-grey dog with sparkling, timid dark eyes, which had come up to them on the steamers' jetty and to whom they'd shown kindness, was following them still. Sometimes he went before them, sometimes he lagged behind, but always he stayed close. Occasionally he stopped right in front of their feet, looked at them and wagged his tail.

"Perhaps he's trying to find someone to take him in," said Tomas. "He's lost his master."

Marta walked on quietly, muttering something to herself.

"Are you reciting something?" asked Tomas.

"Yes," said Marta. "I'm trying to remember an old autumn hymn I learned as a child. It starts like this:

'With hasty course and faded light
The sun bids leave so early
To rise with tardy sombre flight
Once more in heavens cloudy.

The year's fair days have passed away . . .'"

The rest was lost in the wind.

They'd just passed the bridge keeper's little cottage and come down onto Nockeby bridge. The wind was blowing in from the east, and the Mälaren was heaving breakers over the low, floating bridge, which rolled and swayed with the force. The spray burst up high into their faces. Tomas and Marta began to run; in the middle of the bridge was a channel for steamers and a jetty, and at the jetty was one of the Svartsjöland boats, headed for town. They reached it just in time.

The shaggy little dark-grey dog stood alone on the jetty and whimpered softly, its tail between its legs.

*

Tomas was late; the family was just rising from the table when he got home for dinner. Afterwards he drank coffee in his old room. It looked empty now he'd moved the desk and the bookcases to his attic room up by Adolf Fredrik.

Out in the hall Greta stood dressed to go out, inspecting herself in the mirror.

"Where are you off to?" asked Tomas.

"I'm going shopping," replied Greta.

Greta often chose the twilight hour to go looking in the shops. There was something so inviting about the streets as darkness fell and the lamps were being lit. There was so much to marvel at and wonder about.

She gave Tomas a nod from the doorway and disappeared.

Tomas went in to his mother and chatted awhile; but he wasn't minded to sit long: he wanted to go home and read.

He promised to come back for supper.

The sky had cleared as dusk approached, and the wind had fallen. All the day's turbulent clouds had drifted off and melted away; only on the western horizon, behind the bare branches in Humlegården, had some stark cloudbanks stacked themselves up into a sharp-edged, deep-violet wall.

Tomas had been meaning to make his way home through Humlegården when, well up Sturegatan, he saw a slender man in a broad hat approaching, keeping tight to the frontages. Might that be Hall? It was his gait: he walked just like that, brushing along the walls . . . Tomas had heard somewhere that he'd arrived back a week ago, but he'd heard nothing from him, and someone else was now living in his old flat on Kommendörsgatan.

It was him.

"Good evening, Hall. Welcome back!"

"Good evening, Tomas. It's a while since we met . . ."

The two friends walked down Sturegatan together. They talked about this and that they'd done over summer. Tomas, however, could not talk about the most important things that had happened to him, and awareness of the fact made him suspect that Hall too, as he spoke, was avoiding everything of significance. In any case, they didn't have that much to say to one another. Time and again pauses arose in their conversation. Tomas felt almost embarrassed without knowing why, and Hall was uninterested and distracted.

At the junction with Humlegårdsgatan he bid Tomas a brisk farewell; he had to meet such and such and someone else up at the Anglais.

"See you soon, no doubt," he said.

And he gave Tomas his new address.

They shook hands with a warmth that sought to make up what was lacking in their conversation, and Tomas headed off homewards.

Hall didn't go up to the Anglais; he wasn't meeting anyone there.

He had, as sometimes happened to him, merely felt a compelling need to be alone and drift around among people wherever the impulse took him.

The theatres would soon be opening their doors; the streets were crowded.

Hall turned into Birger Jarlsgatan, where the lights were just starting to burn around him, one after another, under an empty blue-green October sky. Over the calm slow waters of Nybroviken wandered the faint green light of a ship, while above Freemasons' House on Blasieholmen — the tall, dark Bååt mansion — a hazy moon slowly rose, its face crooked, as if swollen by toothache.

He hadn't been walking long before he started to feel tired. Should he go home? No, not home . . .

Why would I go home? he thought. *I've nothing to do, and besides, that blank white paper on the desk haunts me. But it has to be there so I have it to hand when I have an idea, because I'm writing a drama, aren't I?*

He walked irresolutely up and down the pavement outside Berzelii Park.

That white paper is my troubled conscience . . .

Still, he had to settle somewhere since he was tired. He went into the bar at Berns, which happened to be nearest, sat in a corner of one of the galleries and ordered a whisky.

A variety show was underway. Onstage a fat lady was jumping around warbling, without however making herself heard above the orchestra and the hubbub of the drinking, smoking and yelling clientele.

Yes, why couldn't he write? He'd seen and done a lot of things, after all. Maybe it was because he lacked the proper childlike faith that he really did have something new to say. And even supposing he did, what then? People still wouldn't listen. It was from the most peculiar nooks and crannies of existence that he drew his experience.

Maybe he didn't have the proper childlike belief in genius

either. What are geniuses? Deft, clever children who attach themselves to the harness of work and whip themselves with those frenzied old dreams of greatness; and with the illusion that greatness is great.

The fat songstress had left the stage; in her place was a middle-aged gentleman who, with the most impassioned contortions of his whole body, was crooning some soppy ballad.

What could he devise to make time soar on eagle's wings rather than creep along like a snail — even if only for a few months?

He wanted to be loved, and yet he feared nothing as much as love. He'd had a few idle dalliances, short and strange, but passion he'd fled like the plague — not that it had exactly sought him out. He loved no one, and no one loved him.

He was the poorest man in the world.

The singer onstage bowed and drew back amid feeble applause. The nobler sentiments could, at this establishment, aspire to no more than a *succès d'estime*.

A few paces from Hall, beneath a chair, sat a fat brown rat nibbling at a lobster shell she was holding in her front paws. When she noticed that Hall was looking at her she momentarily stopped what she was doing and frankly met his gaze with her clever little eyes, glistening black. Then she returned, unperturbed, to her own affairs.

Hall regarded her thoughtfully.

If they have live rats here, they must also have dead ones, because rats do not have eternal life. I wonder, beneath which crack in the floorboards will this one end up lying rotting?

All at once he fancied the whole place infused with the smell of dead rats. He summoned the waiter, paid and headed towards the exit as six girls painted red and white screeched and flapped around onstage in mad confusion, like living dishcloths.

He went out through Berzelii Park, over Norrmalmstorg and came into Biblioteksgatan.

Wasn't that Greta Weber walking in front of him? With the blonde hair just done up in a bun . . .

He caught up with her, greeted her politely and gratefully recalled their last meeting. They hadn't met since sharing a table at the Arvidsons' dinner.

They walked up Östermalm together. Greta behaved rather correctly at first and confined herself to brief replies. But Hall jested in such an open and good-natured way that she soon came to trust him and forgot her reserve, smiling and joking just as he.

Hall was enchanted. He hadn't thought about Greta all summer. How could he not have remembered her and thought about her . . . ?

He spoke of his travels, and Greta attended with keen ears and inquiring eyes.

They'd reached the flower shop on Stureplan; they stopped awhile outside the window looking at the flowers.

"I didn't appreciate orchids at all at first," said Greta. "I thought they looked so strange. But now I like them best of almost all flowers — especially those big pale-green ones that look like sea creatures —"

She'd barely finished her sentence before Hall had vanished into the shop. The next moment he came out with a green orchid in his hand.

Greta blushed.

He wanted to fix it to her bosom, but she, in some alarm, refused it.

"Oh no, you shouldn't have done that — why did you buy it? — no, no I don't want it."

Hall looked stonily at her. Finally he threw the flower away onto the street, in the grime, bid a polite farewell and set off down a side street.

Greta was left standing confused, close to tears.

But she quickly pulled herself together.

Well — wasn't that rather a thing? Or perhaps you couldn't quite call it a thing . . . ?

She looked round in every direction: there was nobody paying her any attention, was there? Then she bent down, picked up the flower, dried it and wrapped it in her handkerchief. It wouldn't do to leave this beautiful, costly flower lying there in the dirt . . .

She wanted to keep it as a memento.

*

Tomas was sitting at the window in his room. He'd left the lamps unlit. He was looking at the rooftops' and the chimneys' darkening silhouettes against the twilight sky, and at a faint star, shining forth through the thinning crowns of the elms. The bare wall opposite, across the courtyard, flared red again and again, a reflection from the smithy's furnace down on the ground floor. The sound of hammer on anvil was all that broke the evening silence out in the yard.

Tomas was thinking about Marta. She'd behaved so strangely this morning; what was troubling her?

Could something have gone wrong? They hadn't always taken precautions . . .

The seamstress in the window across the way now lit her lamp. The glow fell into Tomas's room; he could see the shadow of his own head moving on the wallpaper.

A dark bowed figure with a sack on his back and a stick in his hand crept silently across the courtyard. It was the rag-and-bone man. He padded up to the dustbin, lifted the lid and started poking around inside with his stick; he gathered up a few bones, turned them over, and put them in his sack. Then he put the lid back and crept away again.

The heavy gate shut behind him with a crash.

Still the smith's hammer worked on, and the fire glow on the wall flared ever redder, while the huts and fences in the yard darkened ever more in the October gloom. In a neighbouring yard a dog began to bark — some women were talking and laughing in the entryway — and then they all fell silent again.

Tomas jumped. Someone was knocking on the door.

It was Marta.

"Marta, it's you — I was just sitting here alone in the dark thinking about you, but I wasn't expecting you. You were meant to be going somewhere . . ."

"I know," said Marta, "I've just come from there; it was so dull. I said I didn't feel well and left. Of course they had to find a gentleman to accompany me — that couldn't be avoided. He came as far as the front door to our apartment block, and I waited inside a long time before I dared go out again. And now here I am!"

She put her coat on a chair and stood before him in her white evening gown with its lace sleeves. She hadn't bought herself a new one since spring, but in her sash and in her hair she no longer wore violets, but white roses.

Still she stood erect in the middle of the floor.

"I want to tell you something, Tomas," she said. "I want to tell you why I was crying."

Tomas felt himself going pale.

"I think I'm going to have a child."

Tomas was speechless, standing staring at her as if he didn't understand.

But Marta stood pallid and calm. She wasn't crying now.

"We've done wrong, Tomas; now we shall have to pay."

The hours ran past.

Tomas and Marta could not leave one another. Every second seemed more precious than ever. They felt happiness slipping out of their grasp; they saw her as a capricious, affronted guest, turning her back on them and leaving wide open the door to darkness, the unknown, to misery. They could not repent that they had loved one another, and so instead they regretted every hour they allowed to pass by empty and unused. Their eyes sought one another's with the fire of a passion different than before, their lips burned with an ardour more fervent, and their embraces became convulsive embraces, such as might restrain a flight; and from that day forward they loved the love of those condemned.

XII

The November gloom was deepening over the rooftops and chimneys.

Greta stood at one of the windows in the dining room, looking down at the street and drawing crooked lines with her finger in the condensation that was spreading higher and higher up the glass.

"Look, it's snowing," she said softly, letting her hands fall to her sides. "The first snows of winter!"

There was something reverent in her voice. For a long time she stood in silence, gazing at the snowflakes as they sank down, big, damp snowflakes that made the roofs and the window ledges white and the darkness white.

Tomas was sitting at the piano playing incessantly on a single key; he fancied it gave a softer, less ragged sound than the others.

At last he grew tired of it and silence fell.

Their mother walked through the room. She paused for a moment behind Tomas and gently stroked his hair a few times with one hand. When he turned she nodded to him, bright-eyed, and was gone again.

It was still not six o'clock. At half past he'd have to be at his flat: Marta had promised to come.

Time, it passed so slowly . . .

Still Greta stood slender and erect between the house-plants, close by the window pane, watching the snow fall.

Then suddenly she turned towards Tomas.

"Tomas, tell me: Johannes Hall — is he a good man?"

Tomas didn't answer straightaway. The question came so

unexpectedly.

At last he said, "I think he is. He's certainly a very complicated character, I might add."

Greta stared stubbornly at him, as if demanding he say more; but Tomas remained silent. Finally she suppressed a little yawn and went into her room to stretch out on the bed and sleep awhile, because it was dark and dreary and in any case she was sleepy. These past few weeks she'd been lying awake such a long time at night before she finally fell asleep.

Tomas was left sitting alone at the piano and heard the clock strike six. It struck so slowly and sounded so tired. After the first five tarrying, hesitant strokes Tomas thought it would never reach the sixth.

How it's all aged in here this past year! The clock and the piano and the whole room, everything.

He got up and went out.

The street was already white with snow. Tomas couldn't hear the sound of his own footsteps.

A young workman ran down the street, bellowing with laughter, a couple of Dalecarlian girls in hot pursuit, hands full of powdery snow which they threw over his head and shoulders. Their happy laughter echoed round the walls, grew remote, and was gone.

Tomas still had plenty of time; he took a route along the Esplanade. Snow swirled up and down, sparkling in the blue-white light of the arc lamps.

A cab raced past, conveying a raucous party of ladies and gentlemen. Cries and laughter spilled out along their path, mixed in with the refrain from the latest variety song.

Wasn't that Hall among them? Yes, indeed it was; he'd a decided partiality for lively company nowadays.

Tomas suddenly spotted his father and his uncle, a bookseller in Södermalm, a few steps ahead of him. The two brothers met very rarely, but whenever they did chance to run into one another on some street corner they would always stop and chat awhile.

Tomas swung his umbrella to the other side so he could pass by unnoticed; he'd no wish to be delayed. From the two old gentlemen's conversation he caught only the word 'Helgeandsholmen'.

Coming to that quiet, empty stretch of Karlavägen which runs along the residential district, he cast a passing glance up at the windows of the Arvidsons'. The lights were on in the sitting room. A short square neck could be glimpsed, and nearby the silhouette of a woman, leaning forward, seen against the yellow shade of the standard lamp. Whose neck was that, was it Grothusen's? Yes: Grothusen with Mary Arvidson . . .

He'd lost track of time; the appointed hour had arrived . . .

And he hurried onwards through the snowstorm, his eyes fixed on a patch of light at the end of the road where a street lamp drowsed red on a red placard.

As he was about to go through the street door he was startled by a hand laid on his arm.

"Tomas . . ."

It was Marta.

"Have you been waiting?"

"No, I only just arrived . . . I went up and knocked on your door but nobody answered . . ."

The snow swirled around them. Tomas wanted to kiss her, but she pushed him back and drew away.

"No, I'm not going up again," she said. "I want to go home."

In the darkness Tomas tried to meet her gaze, but it slid off and away.

"But why? Marta . . . don't you feel well, has something happened?"

"No, but I want to go home! I want to go home!"

She was gone, and Tomas stood alone outside the doorway.

What to do? He couldn't bring himself to go upstairs. Up there it was empty and lonely.

And once more he drifted around out in the snow.

*

Marta hurried home. As she stood alone in the dark stairway outside Tomas's door, knocking, waiting and knocking again, despite realising he wasn't there, she had suddenly come to ask herself: Why am I standing here?

And she had no answer. She knew with gnawing certainty that it was over.

And what next?

How different it had all been a year ago! The days of the week glided by, some smiling, some sad, and she worked at her embroidery or read a book and thought about nothing, and sin was something strange and remote that didn't concern her. *This* was right and *that* was wrong. Here was something one ought to do, there, something one would never dream of doing. Everything so clear and simple! And now . . . She no longer knew what right and wrong were. They'd all been mixed up together and become so strange.

But still, was it not something terrible that she'd done, and was it not something terrible that now awaited her?

She was paler than usual when she got home.

The light was on in the drawing room. Mrs Brehm sat in one corner of the pale-red couch reading an English book that she intended to translate; her eyes played, girlishly clear and lively, within her bright little rococo head as she turned page after page. Aunt Marie sat sewing in an armchair. Elsa and Johan were stretched out on the rug in front of the stove, where the last twigs were still glowing feebly, and arguing about religion. Johan was nine years old and no longer believed in anything supernatural.

"Where have you been?" asked Mrs Brehm. "You look tired."

"I just went a walk down Drottninggatan for a breath of fresh air. I'd been sitting inside all day long . . ."

She fetched a book and sat down on the other side of the couch, and the hours passed. Later, once they'd taken their meal and the children had gone to bed, Marta said good night and went to her room.

Mrs Brehm returned to her reading, but she found it hard to concentrate.

What was it Marta spent her days thinking about? Because there was certainly something. She wasn't herself any more.

Mrs Brehm herself didn't know how long she'd been sitting there thinking, the book in her lap, when she heard something like a sob coming from Marta's room. She quickly rose and tiptoed to her door and opened it a crack.

Indeed, Marta was lying awake, crying.

Mrs Brehm sat down cautiously on the edge of the bed and began to stroke her cheek.

"What is it, Marta? Tell me why you're crying. You've been so changed lately. Tell me everything!"

Marta was no longer sobbing. She lay still with her eyes wide open, staring into space. She knew that the time had come for what could not be averted.

And she told all.

Mrs Brehm would not be perturbed. The misfortune summoned up all that was strongest and best in her nature; this was how she was. Long into the night she held counsel with Aunt Marie, and it was agreed that Mrs Brehm and Marta should journey to Norway over the winter.

Mrs Brehm sat in thought even after Aunt Marie had gone

to bed and all was quiet. Time after time she could hear Marta turning in her bed: still, then, she lay awake.

Mrs Brehm went in to her, sat with her and stroked her hair.

"Marta, dear Marta . . ."

And finally she leaned over and whispered quietly, "Marta, tell me, do you know who Aunt Marie is?"

Marta stared at her mother with big, frightened eyes. What new thing was now upon her?

But Mrs Brehm met her eyes calmly in the dark. "She is your grandmother," she said, simply and gently.

*

Tomas wandered round for a long time, and when he'd tired himself out walking he went up to the Anglais.

"Hello there, Gabriel, good evening!"

Mortimer was sitting alone in a corner with a glass of whisky and a newspaper in front of him. He made room for Tomas and Tomas sat down.

He soon had the feeling that Mortimer was looking older than when he'd seen him last.

"So, you've torn yourself away and left your wife alone, what does she have to say about that?"

"She's not alone. There's an old lady at home with her, keeping her company. Dressed in black."

Tomas ordered a whisky.

"I haven't seen you for a long time," said Mortimer.

"I came round the other day but there was nobody home."

"Ah, then that was probably the day before yesterday. My wife had this sudden desire to go to the Södra Theatre the day before yesterday; she reproached me that we hadn't been there for five years. So, well — we went. The play was stupid, but edifying."

"What was it called?"

"That I don't remember. There's this gorgeous adulteress running round in her corset, a respectable older man who's not her husband hopping up and down on one leg in his shirt-sleeves, and then this younger man comes charging out of a very dark side room with a hat on his head and a tailcoat in his hand, while the jealous husband runs round shooting everyone with a gun: Pow! Bang!"

"Is that edifying?"

"Of course! Anything that's meant to make a mockery of love is edifying."

Tomas examined him furtively. Was he drunk? This wasn't his usual face.

"*Faust* is not edifying. It's designed to give young people the idea that love means something."

Three gentlemen who were drinking spirits at a nearby table broke off their conversation and listened to Mortimer's words with that same mixture of admiration and derision with which the uneducated listen to the speech of foreigners. No power on earth can persuade them that anyone could understand a single word of such gibberish.

Tomas thought he knew one of them from the shape of his back, which had made a disagreeable impression on him before.

For a few minutes it fell quiet. Mortimer raised his glass, exchanging a polite greeting with a gentleman sitting alone by the wall opposite — a pale man with large, staring eyes in a slender face with a short dark beard.

"Who's that?" asked Tomas.

Mortimer gave his name and added, "He's a doctor of philosophy, and he spends his time polishing his furniture. When you go to his flat you can see yourself everywhere — in every cupboard, every chest of drawers, every tabletop. Everything is always newly polished and shiny as glass."

"What else does he do?"

"I don't know if he does anything else. Once upon a time there was a young woman who gave him the idea that love meant something. After a while he noticed that this wasn't the case, and now he polishes furniture."

And Mortimer continued with an abrupt transition: "You have to better yourself, Tomas. Attend to your studies, live an honourable life, and stay away from love!"

Tomas blushed deeply. Did Mortimer know something? No — that was unthinkable, of course . . .

"Stay away from love until you have the means to love a woman; love is the preserve of those of us with salaries and dividends. And stay away from it then too!"

Tomas shifted a little uneasily and brought his glass to his lips.

"Cheers!" he said, for the sake of saying something.

He was still irritated by the figure of that back and neck; if only he could catch a glimpse of the face, belonging to . . .

Mortimer sat crumpled up in his corner, silent. Suddenly it was as if he had nothing more to say. There was an extinguished cigarette in the corner of his mouth and now and then he sipped from his glass.

It was midnight; the gaslights were turned down and the bar lay quiet and subdued in the half-light.

Tomas suddenly got the feeling someone was watching him and he looked up. Indeed, the man with the back had turned round and was examining him attentively with two ginger-brown eyes in which something half mocking lay concealed.

The brick merchant . . .

Tomas shook Mortimer's hand and quickly rose.

"Good night," he said, "I'm sleepy."

XIII

Tomas and Marta did not meet again. A week passed without his hearing anything from her, and he couldn't find the resolve to write; nor was she any longer the centre of all his thoughts, something he himself noticed with surprise. He went on as if in a stupor: before him, and all around him, lay a desert of grey indifference, yet he felt that something must soon happen nonetheless. It was a condition that reminded him of a dream he had often had as a child: he was standing on the railway tracks, and far off along a curve he could see the train, he could hear its roar and rattle, and he could see it coming closer, getting bigger and bigger, and he stood there, crippled, unable to move a limb.

But he lived as he had lived before, and let time pass as best it would.

Then one day a messenger came with a letter and a long, rectangular package.

He opened the letter and read.

Tomas —

Yes, it's over. Haven't we long known as much? Tomorrow I'm taking the evening train with mother and going to Norway; I don't know when we'll meet again. I find it strange. I have to travel far away and hide myself; so I must certainly have done something very wrong. We often spoke about that, you and I, and time and again you proved to me, clear as the day, that what we were doing was right. Do you remember that we often talked about it? It was always me who took it up, because I was always troubled — always — when I was alone, even though I was carefree and happy when we were together. And now, writing to you, I'm still trying to remember everything you said; but I can't remember it all, and I'm afraid that it's precisely the most important part that I've forgotten. Are you sure, Tomas, are you really sure that you were right? Because if so then why do I have to travel far away, to another country where nobody knows me, and hide? I don't understand it. I don't understand any of it. I regret it — yes, I regret it bitterly — but I don't know if I'm right to regret it. I don't know anything at all now. Do you remember those days when we'd done nothing but kissed a few times? Those were the happiest days. I had a bad conscience then too and I thought I'd done something very wrong, though no doubt only because it was more fun that way. Those days will never come again — not even in my dreams can I get them back — and I grieve for them. Tomas, when you think about it, don't you wish those days were still with us too? Everything would be so different then.

But it was destined not to be. Instead it is I who am different. Farewell, Tomas! Should I thank you for what has been? That I don't know. Do I still love you? That I dare not even ask myself. But I will never forget you. Farewell!

Marta.

That was all.

For a long time Tomas sat motionless, the letter crumpled in his hands. Finally he burst into tears.

The letter was dated the previous day: this evening, then, she would depart. In an hour's time she'd already be underway.

Suddenly he noticed that he was no longer crying. He couldn't even recall why he'd just been crying. He reread the letter from the beginning, trying to find what had seized him in such a singular way; but he couldn't find it again.

Now, the package . . . what could there be in that rectangular package . . . ?

He tore off the wrapping paper and found himself standing, bewildered, with a tin trumpet in his hands — a little toy trumpet of painted tin, with blue and red stripes round its bell.

The Midsummer gift.

There was nothing about it in the letter: it was clearly an afterthought.

At last he put it to his lips and began to toot. He could get no more than a single note out of it, a veiled, husky note, out of tune.

It had just been raining outside. The streets lay damp and shining, mottled by the darkness of the autumn evening and sparks of light from the gas lamps.

Tomas was headed down towards the railway station; he wanted to see if he could catch a glimpse of Marta in one of the carriage windows.

He was thinking of the closing words of her letter as he walked past a little tearoom in a side street where once, long ago, he'd been with Marta: that was one evening in May, when the cherry trees had just come into bloom . . . he couldn't help but smile, seeing two young people crossing over from the pavement opposite, casting furtive glances all around, and then disappearing through the narrow doorway into the shop, she in front, he behind.

Indeed, now it was someone else's turn. For him and Marta the game was over.

Suddenly it occurred to him that both those figures that had just slipped past him in the darkness were, in fact, very familiar: one reminded him of Johannes Hall, the other of Greta — but of course that was impossible. It must have been his imagination.

He stopped irresolutely before the main steps up to the station; in five minutes the train would be leaving. No, obviously he wouldn't be able to go onto the platform without running into her mother and the other ones . . .

He turned off to the left and walked slowly along the railway bridge.

. . . But just suppose it had been Hall and Greta. Why shouldn't it have been them? Nothing was impossible . . .

An everyday conversation between an old man and his wife, who were walking arm in arm just in front of him, now attracted Tomas's attention and captured his thoughts almost without his noticing. From what they were saying he gathered they had a son, that things were going badly for him at school, that he wanted to leave, and that that was probably for the best. And once he had left, what would he do then? Would he go and work in a shop, or get an office job?

The train rumbled forth and Tomas walked on absentmindedly and didn't notice it until the last carriages had already rolled past.

So she was gone . . .

Tomas stood alone halfway across the railway bridge.

The atmosphere had grown heavy again. From Lake Mälaren came a fog, slowly sailing like an opaque white darkness. He felt as if eternity itself were coming towards him, appallingly wide and empty, annihilating everything around him, swallowing up the buildings and the quays and the gaslights and leaving him alone on a few slippery boards, a castaway on a raft, floating out in space. Only occasionally, when the fog thinned for a moment, could he see a lamp on one of the boats in the harbour casting a pale, threadlike streak of light down into the water.

For a long time he stood straight and motionless, staring out at this pale lonely light, emerging time after time from the void, gleaming for a moment and then dying away.

A dark figure approached slowly and unsteadily through the fog. Just next to Tomas he tripped and fell. Tomas hesitated for a moment, then took him by the arms, helped him up and dusted off his coat. It was an old man; he was drunk and didn't say a word. He tottered off quietly as he came, an indistinct form gliding away and dissolving into nothing. The fog took him, and he was gone.

And once more it was empty and endless, and the lamp on the boat blinked on for a second and was extinguished anew.

Tomas stood as if nailed to the spot, not knowing himself what held him there.

He'd started thinking about Ellen. What had become of her? He'd heard from Hall that she was no longer working at the glove shop.

He turned and took a few steps back in the direction he came.

Right behind him he heard the sound of soft, brisk footsteps, like a young woman's. He'd just reached a lamppost when she caught him up and passed him. In the lamplight he could see it was Ellen.

"Ellen . . ."

It came involuntarily, a half cry he couldn't stifle, and that startled him. She stopped at once and gazed at him for a few moments without saying a word.

Tomas was more confused than she.

"It's been such a long time since we last met. You look pale . . . I'd love to hear how you are, how you've been doing, since we . . ."

He couldn't find the words.

"Thank you, Mr Weber," said Ellen softly, "it's kind of you to ask . . ."

There was no bitterness in her voice, thanking him for his kindness. And she added that she was fairly well, and that she was going to get married the following month.

"You're getting married — who to? Tell me!" said Tomas.

And Ellen explained what had happened, simply and obediently.

She'd made the acquaintance of a watchmaker, who was just about to set up on his own this winter: he planned to start small, but in time the business could grow, if all went well. He wasn't especially young, but he was ever so kind and good and very skilled at his work. She hadn't accepted at once, but afterwards, thinking about it carefully, she'd realised she could hardly do better than to say yes, because she didn't want to become a bad girl. Besides, he liked her very much and had promised to make her happy; he was a hunchback, though.

XIV

There was darkness and snow and rain and one dreary grey day followed close on another, as the city sank deeper and deeper into the December twilight.

Fleeing loneliness and his own thoughts Tomas Weber lived as a man ought not to live.

One morning when he awoke — not so very early — he found a letter on his desk; the landlady had presumably left it there while he slept. Its outer appearance was as inscrutable as a love letter's, the inscription made with pedantic care. He opened it and read.

It was from the brick merchant. He merely wished to remind Tomas that repayment was now already a number of days overdue. The matter must be resolved by three o'clock today; otherwise he would regrettably be obliged to apply without further delay to one of the guarantors for recovery of the sum outstanding. Yours faithfully . . .

Already? How could this be . . . ?

Tomas cast a glance in the mirror: he was pale and grey. Then he quickly got dressed and went out.

He wanted to find Hall. He was sure Hall could help him, and that he wouldn't refuse.

Where was it he lived? Wasn't it somewhere up by Östermalm church?

It was a pity they'd spent so little time together recently.

A fine sleety rain was falling, melting the snow on the streets. The buildings in the narrow alleys between Adolf Fredrik Church and Hötorget huddled together, shy and shabby, with mottled, pockmarked walls, blackened by rain, dripping with damp and dirt. The sky was a single dense yellow-grey fog. People walked like sleepwalkers, seeing nothing; the sleet whipped at their faces and flakes fastened on eyelashes. Time and again the hum of the streets was pierced by a long muffled roar, as if from some enormous ravenous beast. Tomas had noticed it constantly these past days: it was the sound of a foghorn being tested at some engineering works out on Kungsholmen. Everywhere, in every part of the city, you could hear it all day long, just as loud, just as menacingly close.

Tomas headed through the Brunkeberg Tunnel. Even there, deep in the bowels of the earth, where the lamplight glistened yellow-red over slimy, dripping walls, the horn's hungry roar pursued him.

He practically ran through Humlegården and Östermalm. It was in Jungfrugatan that Hall lived. Tomas dashed up the stairs and rang the bell.

Nobody answered.

He rang again, louder. Finally he rang a third time, rang like a man possessed, and found himself standing there with the bell pull in his hand; he'd torn it off.

Inside the flat all was quiet as ever; no footsteps could be heard coming to the door.

Why wasn't he answering? Was he dead?

Suddenly it occurred to him that most likely Hall was not at home.

Tired and confused he tossed the bell pull off into a corner and walked slowly down the stairs.

Straight ahead of him, at the end of the street, the dark-green bell-shaped dome of Östermalm church loomed out of the haze of snow. Tomas stared in amazement at the clock face on the tower: it was showing half past one. And he'd only just got up, he'd been sleeping so long . . .

He walked on down the street, lost in thought. The bells

in the tower rang, and human silhouettes milled round one another down in the church doorway. Perhaps there was a funeral.

Indeed, he'd been sleeping far, far too long . . .

The church bells rang, but not in their usual way; when they rang the earth rocked and the air sang and the buildings tottered hither and thither like drunkards. And was it just the bells ringing, wasn't it the whole dome itself? Wasn't that whole dark, heavy dome moving slowly back and forth like the monster bell of a swinging cathedral?

Indeed it was swaying menacingly back and forth, thundering, resounding, ringing in Judgement Day, and not a moment too soon, men had sinned quite enough already . . . And there was a crush of people round the steps in the church-yard. A cabbie cracked his whip, and a frenzied grey horse reared up over the crowd, whinnying, its front legs flailing, and the cabbie cracked his whip and cursed. In every doorway women stood with eyes wide open and whispered, holding gaping children by the hand, and eight drunken old men dressed in black with white cotton gloves walked in rows, two by two, bearing a black coffin, their backs curved like worms under the weight.

And high above them all swung a giant clangorous soot-black bell that thundered and resounded, and the horse reared . . .

No, on, onwards . . . He was in no mood to stand watching a funeral procession today, onwards as fast as can be; he almost slipped on the spruce twigs. The thunder of the bells pursued him, and the foghorn began to bellow anew.

Tomas had made for Kungsträdgården. The snow was falling denser and softer, muffling the din around him. He felt calmer.

He decided to go up and see Gabriel Mortimer. He wanted to tell him the whole story from beginning to end, hiding nothing; then Mortimer would surely help him if he could: anything else was unthinkable.

He went straight down Hamngatan and turned off into Västra Trädgårdsgatan to avoid the big noisy thoroughfares. Like a criminal who at any moment might expect to be seized and dragged off to prison he crept along, shadowing the smooth grey walls of the aristocrats' houses. To the left lay St Jacob's churchyard, quiet and empty, white with newly fallen snow. Tomas crossed the street and looked in through the railings. There was a stone bench just next to the church wall. Once inside, he could sit on that bench as long as he wanted and rest.

And for longer than he knew himself he leant against the railings, staring in at this shielded and secluded nook which in the middle of a bustling city was never trampled by the processions that thronged the streets, and where bare slender poplars struck a silent circle round the graves.

But then once again the air shook with the same muffled hungry roar. Tomas woke from his daydream, tore himself away and hurried on in his hunt for money.

Money . . . he might be ready to sell his soul for money.

Already he stood outside Mortimer's door, and already he'd pressed the doorbell, when the simple fact struck him that of course Mortimer couldn't possibly be at home; he was always in the office at this time of the day. But he'd already rung, and there were footsteps approaching — what could he say?

It was Mrs Mortimer herself who answered.

In fact Gabriel was at home; but he was ill.

Tomas was startled.

"How long has he been ill? Is it serious?"

"It is; he's very ill. He's in dreadful pain; sometimes it affects his mind."

As they were speaking Tomas came through into the

drawing room. The elderly lady dressed in black was sitting on a chair by the window darning socks.

"He's been in bed since the day before yesterday," Mrs Mortimer continued in a hushed voice. "The doctor thinks it's appendicitis, but he still can't be sure."

Tomas stood in silence. He couldn't think of anything appropriate to say.

A pause. Through the closed door to the sickroom came a faint moan that rose and fell and occasionally intensified to a stifled cry.

"And I suppose I can't go in to him . . ."

In fact Tomas had no desire at all to go in and see the sick man; on the contrary, he instinctively withdrew ever closer to the front door.

"No, no certainly not; nobody's allowed in but me."

The old lady, who all the time had been sitting in complete silence darning her socks, now looked up with a moist, wavering gaze behind her glasses.

"No," she said, "he can't bear to see anyone, not even me, whom he's always liked so much and always been so kind to. It's so awful how illness can change a person!"

"Yes," said Tomas, "it is awful."

He had by degrees made his way to the front door, closely followed by Mrs Mortimer, who was talking almost constantly and was in the habit of standing extremely close to anyone she was talking to. Quite unconsciously she'd lapsed into her usual cheerful and chattery conversational tone and was asking Tomas a host of trivial questions about his mother and sister.

Suddenly she interrupted herself in the middle of a sentence and fell silent; inside the sick man was raving. The old woman opened the door a crack and listened attentively.

"He thinks he's off travelling," she whispered. "And he says he's forgotten where it was he was meaning to go . . . and he doesn't know where it is that he's arrived . . ."

And then all was quiet in the sickroom again.

Mrs Mortimer began to sob. Tomas pressed her hand and bid farewell, having mumbled a hope that her husband would soon be restored to health; then he made a deep bow to the old woman and left.

Only on the way down the stairs did he recall that it was his last hope of salvation that had just vanished like a morning mist.

The snowstorm had worsened; the sky was growing ever darker, and dusk began to fall over the streets and squares.

Tomas was dead tired, but still he drifted up and down the streets.

Of course there was still a chance he might run into Hall. He'd often done so just around this time, around lunchtime; what was there to stop them meeting today, when he needed him?

Drottninggatan was teeming with people. Naturally: it was getting on for Christmas. It would be Christmas in a few days' time. In every shop the gaslights were lit, as they had been all day. The windows cast yellow patches of light out over the snow and over the wet asphalt of the pavement. The tramping of feet, the peal of church bells and the clatter of vehicles mingled with the cries of the cabbies and the jingling bells of trams, and through it all came the muffled groaning of the foghorn.

And everyone was out and about in town; one familiar face after another passed him by in the throng.

But Hall, where was Hall . . . ?

Jean Arvidson swept past in a cab; he always took a cab these days. A while ago he'd detached his business dealings from his father's and was now busy setting up a firm of his own.

Suddenly Tomas felt someone take him by the arm; it was Anton Recke. They walked a little way up Drottninggatan together, though Recke was in a hurry and more ran than walked.

"Where were you yesterday? I wanted you to come with me to Berns, there's a new diva there who's quite exceptional . . . The audience stamped their feet and fifty rats were inadvertently killed . . ."

And he disappeared inside a house.

In the middle of the street a little black dog with a drooping tail was running hither and thither in a zigzag, nosing around for a trail he'd lost. Suddenly he vanished under the wheels of a brewery cart that was rattling on down the road. And when the cart was gone and the dog came into view once more, he stood silently for a moment, motionless, one smashed paw raised off the ground, till suddenly the pain hit him and he grasped what had happened and began to howl, a shrill, monotone, rending howl. And people stopped and began staring at him, and the animal didn't move from the spot but just howled and cried . . . until at last a man stepped forward out of the crowd, an old diplomat with a sagging face and a slender waxed moustache. He bent down and picked up the little dog from the street and held him in his arms and stroked him, and the dog whimpered. He stood there in the middle of the street, not knowing what to do, with someone else's run-over dog in his arms — for it could hardly be his own, it was one of those shaggy little dogs that poor old ladies have — stood there not knowing what to do or where to go, until at last an uncouth voice yelled, "Watch out!" and he threw himself aside with the dog in his arms, still whining and crying, and vanished in the throng.

Tomas stood there watching him, pale and scared, till the jostling of passers-by woke him and the flow of people carried him off.

Where was Hall today . . . ?

On the pavement opposite, Grothusen was walking arm in

arm with Mary Arvidson. They'd recently got engaged and
Tomas had forgotten to send a card . . . And Lieutenant Gabel
was also with them, to Mary's right, talking animatedly, while
Grothusen was reserved, proper and silent.

A little way after them came Mrs Wenschen and her husband; he was half a step behind her, as she was walking so fast
he could hardly keep up.

It seemed to Tomas that Mrs Wenschen had grown old.
Her skin had started to sag, she no longer dressed with the
same care and she no longer seemed as irrepressibly lively and
cheerful as before.

He turned round and headed downhill. Down on Fredsgatan or in Gustav Adolf Square he'd definitely run into Hall,
and it was still not too late, still the whole thing could be
sorted out, one way or another, even if the whole sum couldn't
be paid at once.

Mrs Grenholm was walking in front of him all the way
down Drottninggatan. Her backside bobbed up and down so
extravagantly as to hint at the early stages of megalomania: for
the extraordinary had indeed recently come to pass: on one and
the same day Mr Grenholm had been awarded the Order of
Vasa and Dr Rehn the Polar Star.

Tomas's spirits suddenly rose so high it was all he could
do not to burst out laughing. He was almost tempted to go up
to Mrs Grenholm and congratulate her on both these honours.

He was now just as sure of seeing Hall on Gustav Adolf
Square as if the two had already agreed a meeting under Tornberg's clock.

Every now and then he'd stop in front of a shop window.
In one a quaint little replica caught his eye; he immediately
decided to buy it as a Christmas present for Greta, and went
into the shop. Just before the door was a tall narrow mirror; he
shuddered when he caught sight of himself there. His face was
grey and his clothes were spattered with grime and he was

unshaven. Up at the counter there was a crowd of customers, and the shop assistants ignored him. At once he turned round and left.

The snow had almost stopped, the fog banks had lifted and fraying clouds slid slowly away over rooftops and gables.

Tomas had stopped at the junction with Fredsgatan and was looking out into the empty backdrop where the Mälaren flows into the twilight as a broad, blue-black band. And farthest off, slumbering in the grey haze of the winter dusk, you could just see a quiet and desolate shoreline, with flecks of snow among the rocky peaks.

But all around him the streets clattered fervently as ever, and the foghorn growled as hungrily, and the clock struck three.

Three o'clock. And of course he had to meet Hall under Tornberg's clock . . .

He turned up Fredsgatan and dashed ahead without looking where he was going. Suddenly he crashed into someone: a very tall elderly gentleman in furs, for whom everyone else was making way with bared heads and low bows. It was the King; the collision had knocked his hat to one side; it was almost falling off. General Kurck and the Keeper of the Royal Parks stared dumbfounded at Tomas, who mumbled a confused 'sorry' and vanished into the crush.

The darkness deepened more and more, and a little man in a woolly hat went round with quick steps and a crooked back lighting the gas lamps.

Tomas had reached a backstreet, sparsely peopled and with sleepily lit shops.

He'd not found Hall on Gustav Adolf Square, and he had grasped that there was no more hope with him.

How could he have let things go the way they'd gone? It was unfathomable, and now it was too late to brood about it.

His legs would hardly carry him any longer. He felt

threadbare, rejected, spent. Besides, he was hungry, and dinner would be waiting for him at home.

Weariness made him pause in front of every other shop window. At one, where gas flames flapped their reddish light over long rows of second-hand men's clothing, Tomas stood for a long time, staring without a thought in his head at a pair of light-grey trousers, a dash of garishly bold elegance among the other more reticent charcoal-grey or tobacco-brown garments. They had clearly always been an unusually extravagant pair, harlequin checks running obliquely, with broad black seams running down the sides. Tomas felt he'd seen them before. The longer he looked, the more certain he became that they were Gabel's trousers.

So then, home . . .

On his way home he bought himself a gun.

*

Consul Arvidson sat in his office in his private reception rooms looking through his latest post. The large mahogany desk before him was cluttered with books, pamphlets and papers, an illuminated reading lamp with a blue-green globe, a telephone and a bottle of port with a half-empty glass.

There was a quiet knock at the door, which stood ajar. Without looking up the consul called, "Come in!" and Karl Hammer entered.

"There's a gentleman to see you, sir. This is his card. He says it concerns an extremely important matter."

Consul Arvidson took the card Hammer offered him and, with knitted brows, saw the name of a brick merchant, familiar to him from the dealings of others', with whom he neither had nor wanted any dealings himself.

"Show him in."

The brick merchant was already standing in the doorway,

bowing. He bowed again in the middle of the room. When he reached the desk he bowed a third time and presented a piece of paper.

For a long time Consul Arvidson held it in his hand, examining it without saying a word, firstly without his pince-nez, and then with his pince-nez. Finally he let go of the pince-nez, but still scrutinised the document without moving a muscle.

The brick merchant shifted and coughed a couple of times.

The silence began to feel oppressive.

"I hope everything is in order," he said at last. "Or might there perhaps be some irregularity?" he added with a timid attempt at a grin.

The consul produced a box in which he kept a number of loose banknotes and handed over the specified sum.

"Mind your words," he said quietly and flatly. "The document is entirely in order. Good day."

The brick merchant bowed slightly, courteously, and left.

Consul Arvidson sat in thought for a long time, the document in his hand.

He still couldn't believe his eyes.

"Thérèse Weber's son," he murmured to himself. And he repeated it again and again, drumming his fingers on the desk: "Thérèse Weber's son . . ."

Finally he folded the document carefully into four equal parts, cut along the folds with a paper knife and put the pieces in his wallet. Then he emptied his glass, filled it up to the brim with dark-red port and emptied it again in a single gulp.

*

Johannes Hall was walking back and forth in his two-room flat, smoking. Occasionally he stood still, listening for footsteps on the stairs.

The blinds were pulled down, and a healthy fire flickered in the hearth. His desk lamp was outside, illuminating the entrance hall.

He was waiting for Greta. She'd promised to come over for a chat and to look at photographs from his travels and at his collection of etchings based on a number of curious and remarkable pictures.

But would she actually come?

She was so unpredictable. He'd kissed her once — one single time — in a tearoom one afternoon; but since then she'd been so reserved, so quick to take flight.

Hall went to the window and lifted up the blinds a little to look out. It was snowing again, and the wind was whistling round the edges of the buildings. An old lady sailed slowly along the street, the wind behind her, her round-cut coat spreadeagled by the gusts, an umbrella behind her neck.

There she goes, thinking it's all hunky-dory with her rotten old head sheltered from the wind, holding her umbrella so steady behind her neck like that — but now she's reached the corner, and the gust's hit her, and the snow's whipping her in the face and the umbrella's turned inside out . . . and now she's slipped over into the bargain — there she is now, sitting there . . . You help her up if you like, I won't — I'm all right, Jack . . .

He let the blinds fall back down and threw his cigarette away.

She promised she'd be here at six thirty and it's six forty-five already. She's not coming . . .

He stretched out on the couch and burrowed his head in a cushion.

Such a long time to wait . . . And I've waited more than enough already, I've been waiting all my life.

He'd longed for passion, yet had fled from it. But no more! He wanted to know what it meant to love — and to be loved. The time might be ripe.

But could he take responsibility for leading a child to ruin?

Responsibility . . . My father, whom I've never met, he didn't trouble himself with questions of responsibility. I've got family traditions of my own . . .

Responsibility . . . We don't know ourselves what seeds we sow. We can't assume responsibility for anything at all, not for pressing on, or for turning back, or for standing still.

Well now . . . isn't that someone coming up the stairs?

He jumped up from the couch and opened the front door.

Greta stood outside, cheeks red from the wind, shoulders white with snow.

Greta sat on the side of the couch nearest the fire, and Hall sat next to her with a large portfolio in his lap, out of which he produced photographs, etchings and gravures. Greta took them one after another and looked at them silently and distractedly by the light of the lamp's orange shade. Before them stood a little table with a bottle of curaçao and a cigarette case.

"I'm so glad you came," whispered Hall. "You took so long, and I was so lonely."

"Yes . . . I didn't really know whether I should come. But of course I really wanted to see your pictures."

"You can't imagine how grateful I am for your interest in art," said Hall, without smiling.

The next moment he regretted what he'd said; perhaps he'd offended her. But he soon saw his fears were groundless; Greta's ear for irony was not well developed. Hall offered her a cigarette, and she took it without long hesitation.

"This isn't the first time I've smoked," she said. "It's something I learned at school; me and another girl — we were the worst smokers in the whole class."

"Surely not . . ."

And as he lit her cigarette his eyes caressed her downy

cheeks, her slender neck, and the whole of her soft, delicate figure, sharply defined by a tight, smooth dark woollen dress.

The fire crackled in the hearth and outside the wind whistled round the buildings.

Greta looked up from the photographs, sipped her curaçao and took a puff of the cigarette. She felt very content and thought herself rather splendid. How silly she'd been, pacing around at home hesitating, wondering whether she dare come! It wasn't perilous at all. True, it was a little inappropriate, but what did that matter, when nobody would ever know? And in any case you sometimes had to be bold and defy convention.

She was truly proud of herself as she sat there, lounging back on the couch and smiling and taking long drags on her cigarette.

"Look," said Hall, "here comes my *pièce de résistance*."

And he handed her a large album of reproductions after the work of Franz Stuck.

Greta browsed through the book in some amazement. The pictures were so strange, unlike anything she'd ever seen before. She didn't understand them at all, but didn't dare say so openly: then he'd think she was stupid, and that, at any rate, she was not, no matter how badly things had generally gone at school . . .

"Yikes!" she cried, half involuntarily, when she caught sight of a hideous picture, beneath which stood the title *Lucifer*. Lucifer — wasn't that the Devil himself? That couldn't possibly be a subject for a respected artist to tackle nowadays; although of course back in the day anything was fair game . . .

Hall had an inkling that Greta was less than ideally receptive to Stuck's art. He turned over a few pages at once and showed her a picture that bore the title *Es war einmal*.

Greta looked at it for a long time, at first astonished, then rather taken. She felt she understood it better and better the longer she looked.

Once upon a time . . .

. . . on a meadow beneath a yellow-red twilight, an enchanted twilight, there stood a slender princess dressed in white, leaning over something down there in the grass. She bends down, listening with wide frightened eyes and parted lips, but her eyes are somehow smiling too, and she's holding up the edge of her long dress, and she's afraid lest she get her little feet wet, standing there on a tussock. What is it down there in the wet, marshy grass, and what is it that she's hearing, what is she listening to? In the grass by her feet sits a little ugly green frog, looking at her with big, wise, melancholy eyes. And you can see at once that this can be no ordinary frog; or rather, you apprehend it from something secret and sorrowful in his eyes. He has something to tell her, something none shall hear but the princess alone, and the white princess bows down and listens, smiling and afraid. The wind has fallen silent, the better for her to hear. The grass rustles no more, and the boughs of the trees arch unmoving up over the horizon. And all around them the evening stands vast and quiet in that yellow-red enchanted twilight.

Once upon a time . . .

Greta sat with parted lips, smiling and afraid, like the princess herself. She couldn't take her eyes off the picture.

"I'm sure it's a bewitched prince," she said softly.

"Yes," whispered Hall, "and he's asking her to release him from the spell, and she's nodding her head, giving him her word. He's whispering to her, telling her what she must do to make him a prince again, and she's standing there in wonder, and listening, and trembling and smiling. And she becomes frightened and pale, and she's sweeping that white dress tight around herself, and she can never believe she'll dare do what he's saying, because it's something so peculiar, what he's entreating her to do, looking at her with those big eyes, big and wide with a secret sorrow."

Greta had tears in her eyes. Hall added softly: "But perhaps, after all, she will do it just once."

"Yes, perhaps . . ."

The bloom of the fairytale and the sheen of adventure hovered over the picture, over her and everything around her. The enchanted yellow-red twilight became one with the faint light spreading through the orange-yellow shade of the lamp. The brown drink she sipped teased her palette with its sweet, spicy taste and subdued her into a pleasant, dreamy confusion. The cigarette smoke wrapped a thin blue veil around her head and his, as he sat by her side. In the hearth the last embers flared up with a flickering pale-yellow flame, twisting and twirling into curves, reflecting in the smooth planes of polished wood. And she did not tear herself away, or even lean aside, when Hall softly drew her head in to his chest, caressed her hair, kissed her cheek.

"No, no . . ." she mumbled, barely audibly, unmoving, eyes closed. She felt herself lacking all power. She just trembled once or twice, shut her eyes again and dreamed herself into the world of the fairytale: that was where she wanted to be, where she longed to go, where she would follow at the slightest lead. And if now the time had come, she would not hesitate. She wanted to do what he asked of her, the one who sat by her side: everything those strangely roving eyes asked of her, she wanted to do. And though she trembled she was not afraid. If now it happened, this great and wonderful thing that she had never dared tell anyone she longed for . . . this, which the fairytales whispered of, secretly, furtively, this, which was the heart of every beautiful poem . . .

She startled at the sudden violent ringing of the doorbell.

"It's ringing," she whispered in alarm, writhing out of his embrace.

Hall sat motionless, teeth clenched.

"Let it ring, I'm not answering. I'm not at home."

They sat in silence, listening tensely as second followed upon second.

Suddenly the bell rang again, more violently than before, loud enough to wake the dead.

Greta had gone pale.

"You must find out what it is: the building might be on fire."

Hall rose reluctantly and went out on tiptoe into the entryway. He didn't open the door, but looked out through the little window: he was in darkness but the stairwell outside was illuminated, so he could see without being seen.

Tomas Weber was standing outside. He was still waiting, his expression tense, but he didn't ring again. When nobody opened the door he finally went slowly down the stairs.

Tomas. What could he want? He didn't look himself . . .

Hall went back in.

He sat in the same place as before, next to Greta, but he could see the change in her at once. He saw she'd turned over a leaf in the book; and she was not as she had been before.

"No," he said anxiously, wanting to snatch the book from her hands, "you mustn't look at that one, you mustn't! You see — I've put a bookmark there, a pressed flower of henbane: that means we have to skip the page!"

"But," said Greta, "I want to see, I must . . . and I already have . . ."

And she was staring, pale, at a dark image with a dark-green tint.

What was it? The title was *die Sünde*.

Sin . . .

There was a woman. Her hair was dark and her eyes were like two deep wells, and she was naked. Was there ever a woman as naked as she? Her nakedness shone out of the darkness. Around her greenish-white body was coiled a thick, scaly snake. Slippery and cold it slithered forth from between her splayed legs, wound itself up over her shoulders and curled itself in a fat, glistening ring around her neck, its head, with its two glowing green eyes, hanging down between her tumescent breasts. And her hand caressed the snake, dreamily caressed his back and his slender, pointed head. Her eyes were two pits, cold as night, and she was nakeder than any woman could be.

Where was the bloom of the fairytale, where the sheen of poetry and adventure?

Sin . . .

Greta rose from the couch, white with fear. She almost knocked over the little table with the bottle and the glasses.

"I want to go," she said, "I want to go!"

She was in the hallway already, gathering her clothes in the dark and putting them on in a feverish hurry. Hall couldn't calm her: fear had taken her over.

"I want to go," she repeated, her voice trembling. She could utter no other words than these.

She was gone, and Hall stood alone in the room. He looked at his watch: only a little after half past seven.

Time, it passes so slowly . . .

The album lay on the floor, open at the same page. The snake coiled just as scaly and fat around the same greenish-white woman, and her nakedness shone.

*

Tomas stayed at home for a long time after dinner, long after the coffee had been drunk and the cigars burned out.

He was in no hurry any more.

The rooms were so empty. Greta was out — probably looking for Christmas presents in the shops — and father was at a shareholders' meeting.

Where was mother?

He found her in the bedroom; she was reading from Thomas à Kempis, 'Of last and final things'.

Tomas sat down beside her without a word, and she read aloud to him in a soft, gentle voice.

"'O foolish one, why do you not look forward and prepare yourself for the day of judgement, when none may excuse or defend another, but each must bear the weight of his burden alone? The more you now tend yourself and heed the call of the flesh, the worse will be your torments then, and the more you hoard that then will be burned. And there is no guilt that will not then meet its proper torment.'"

Tomas heard, and yet did not listen. He leant over his mother's shoulders and looked at the woodcuts depicting the end of days.

"'What does it serve to live a long life, when so few amend their ways? Alas, a long life does not always a better man make, but often increases his guilt.'"

The last day, the resurrection of the dead . . . would that day really dawn, or was it just a fairytale?

The graves opened, vaults that had stood a thousand years fell, and the white light of the last day streamed in, where before all was dark. The earth spewed forth corpses from its bowels, and the corpses came to life: hands groped and eyes stared, and one of them stood erect already, dazed with sleep and blinded with light, hands before eyes: the sun, the sea!

"You're not listening," said his mother quietly. "You're thinking about something else."

"I am listening . . ."

And she carried on reading, till Tomas suddenly rose, took her hand, stroked it, kissed it.

'Good night' was all he said.

His voice was veiled; he felt as if a sob would break through.

And he went.

His mother sat alone in thought, letting the book fall into

her lap. Tomas had never been in the habit of kissing her hand before.

Tomas went out in the snow.

The words of the old mystic were still ringing in his ears.

'What does it serve to live a long life, when so few amend their ways?'

But no — it couldn't be that it was already over for him. He was so young, he'd only just passed twenty. He was so very young, and there was still so much to do that had not been done.

There must be some recourse. Was there nobody to advise him, nobody who would help him?

Perhaps Hall was home now. It might already be too late, but in any case he wanted to talk to him.

He stopped outside the street door where Hall lived, looking up at his window, and already began to take new heart as he saw light in the cracks round the curtains. He dashed up the stairway and rang. What did it mean that nobody came to answer? He was obviously at home, there was light in the window ...

And when he went down the stairs again he knew that all hope was lost.

His room was cold when he came home. He asked the landlady to make a fire. She'd already made his bed, thinking he'd be back late as usual.

Tomas pulled a chair up to the stove and warmed his feet.

He was freezing.

Still it snowed, and through the snow the red glare from the smithy shone on the wall across the yard and the blacksmith's hammer pounded ceaselessly on as usual. The wind whistled in every crack, and now and then it clattered the window panes.

It was strange how he could never get warm this evening.

Tomas hunted out a bottle of Madeira. It was left over

from the days when Marta would come here. He immediately emptied two glasses, one after the other, and warmed a little.

Ah, Marta . . . was he in her thoughts this evening?

He sat playing with the revolver. An odd little thing . . .

Did he really mean to die here, this very evening?

He did; he no longer saw another way out. He'd been living with his eyes closed. Perhaps it was a dream, everything he'd seen and done, a ghastly, confused dream, and the shot would wake him. Yes, it would be best that way. 'What does it serve to live a long life, when so few amend their ways?'

He understood nothing in his life, now, thinking back on it. It was like dreaming: you walk up the street, down the street, as if you have important business to do, you go into and out of strange buildings, you take part in the most absurd and pointless scenes, and you find it all perfectly natural and proper and you let nothing surprise you. And then you wake up and try to remember what it was you dreamt and find some meaning in it, and then it's all a load of nonsense without the least point or substance.

Oh, how he longed to wake up, once and for all!

But suppose he'd been deceived: suppose nothing but the void awaited him — a dark hole in the earth and nothing more? Or suppose there'd be a reckoning, suppose he'd be held to account for having dreamed his life away in such a stupid and useless dream?

Yes, it was this last thing he was afraid of. Actually he'd probably been no worse than most, and no doubt had done some good things too . . .

Hmm, what, exactly?

And he started to reflect. He was convinced that he had, in actual fact, performed a great many good deeds, although just at the moment he was unable to remember very many of them. Still, he ought to be able to recall at least one. Odd . . . No matter how he delved into his past he found nothing praiseworthy, not the least thing, except that once, last year, he'd given an indigent an old winter coat. But of course it wasn't Tomas himself but his father who paid for his clothes; in point of fact, then, the coat wasn't his to give. In any case, he knew perfectly well that a couple of days beforehand his father had said that the coat could be repaired, while Tomas would have much preferred a new one. Most likely that was the actual reason he'd given it to the beggar.

Strange, anyway . . . could he really not find one single good deed in his life?

He dried the cold sweat from his brow and banished the thought with a shrug of the shoulders.

Maybe he should light the lamp and write some letters?

No: no letters, no explanations. It'll have happened in a moment of madness; everyone would probably be happier that way.

The fire had burned out; the building had fallen quiet. The smith's hammer had wearied, and the glow from his forge no longer flared from the opposite wall.

The courtyard was asleep in the winter darkness.

Tomas was tired. He decided to undress and go to bed.

Now, if he could only get to sleep, and if someone could shoot him while he slept . . . The faint suspicion started to dawn that it was perhaps not, after all, quite such a simple matter as he'd thought to hold a revolver steady in one's hand and pull the trigger and shoot a ball of lead through one's own brain . . .

He undressed in the dark, pulled down the blinds and huddled up in bed.

So now it was time. Was there any way of putting it off any longer?

Well, there were still a few glasses of Madeira left in the bottle . . .

And he slowly drained glass after glass. The sweet, warming wine raised his spirits and made him see everything in a different light. What sort of a ridiculous fantasy was this that had just been tormenting him — that his life had been meaningless and bad? Those spring days with Ellen, the summer with Marta: oh no, nobody could call those things meaningless. If all that was meaningless, what would you say about people who spent their lives in the civil service, or in some clerical work, or standing up in front of a blackboard spouting nonsense — like his father for example? No, he, Tomas, was the one who was right: he had not lived like a fool, but a wise man, and like a wise man he would die!

And with shaking hands he fumbled on the blanket for the revolver, rose where he lay, aimed haphazardly at his head and pulled the trigger.

After a while he came to. He groped around his head with both hands but couldn't feel any wound. Still, there was something wet on the pillow, it could only be blood . . .

The wine had made his head heavy; he fell back against the pillow and lapsed into a deep sleep.

XV

The bells of Adolf Fredrik's were striking ten when Consul Arvidson walked into the old, dilapidated building where Tomas Weber lived. The landlady explained that he was probably still asleep, because he never usually got up so early, and she knocked quietly a couple of times on his door. When the door remained closed, and no sound came from within, the consul himself turned the key and strode in without further ado. It was dark inside; a band of feeble December daylight entered through a large tear in the tatty blinds, illuminating the dust on the writing desk. The consul headed straight for the window and rolled the blinds with such force they clattered open. The pale grey light of morning flooded in, cold and raw. Then he took out his wallet, found the dissected document and turned to face the room.

Tomas was woken by the rattle of the blinds and rose startled in his bed, eyes wide open.

Was he awake? Was he alive? Oh yes: that was the light of day blazing into his eyes . . .

"Good morning," said the consul drily.

Tomas stared at him without reply. Still he had grasped nothing, still he didn't recognise this unknown gentleman standing in the middle of the room with some white paper in his hand, looking for a place to lay his hat. Finally he put it on his head: there was thick dust everywhere.

"Good morning," mumbled Tomas at last, almost as if in sleep.

"Have a look at this," the consul continued in the same dry tone, as he threw the bits of paper onto the bedside table.

"It's an old contract; I daresay you'll be glad of the chance to burn it.

"It's not for your sake I honoured it," he added quietly, pointedly.

Tomas lay there, eyes closed, and was silent. He'd remembered everything; he understood.

"Perhaps there are several such notes of yours in circulation?"

"No."

"Hmm. One is more than enough."

Suddenly it struck him that there was something amiss with Tomas, something peculiar about his appearance.

"What's that scratch you've got on your cheek? How did that get there? And there's blood on the pillow . . ."

Tomas ran his hand over his cheek. He felt his fingers tracing over a slippery plug of congealed blood.

He suddenly recalled the failed gunshot and blushed deeply. Evidently the bullet had just grazed his cheek . . .

"You'll be wanting to clean that up; it looks uncomfortable."

The consul abruptly fell silent: he'd stepped on something on the floor. A gun . . . What was this about? A gun on the floor . . . And, looking once more at Tomas, lying there dark red with shame, not daring to open his eyes, he couldn't help but feel pity for him. He was young, he'd got himself lost in one labyrinth or another and hadn't thought he could find the way out except like this: so he'd seized on this tired old expedient and gone and pulled the trigger like an idiot . . .

Now the consul had grown annoyed at his own sentimentality. One corner of his mouth turned down to a cold, contemptuous sneer. With one foot he kicked the revolver, sending it far underneath the bed, and left without another word.

Still Tomas lay there with eyes shut, and eventually he

fell asleep again. He dreamt he was out walking in a wood, which was like a park, and a girl was walking by his side. She wore a pale-coloured dress with lace sleeves, and in the sash round her waist was a bunch of violets. It was Marta, and yet it wasn't really her. No, it couldn't be her . . . Marta didn't have such yellow teeth and sagging skin, and her smile was never so brash and lewd. And yet it was her, because it was her voice: Catch me if you can! And then she started to run, but very slowly; she ran with little short steps and all the time she would be turning to him and smiling and showing her yellow teeth. How it tormented him, this grin of hers; but of course when she offered he had to follow . . . And so he sped his steps and pretended to run and strove to smile as she smiled, but only out of politeness. Finally she ran into a bosquet of manicured hedges and once there she turned and stuck her head round the corner of a hedge and waved and smiled and winked in a way Marta would never have done. But Tomas pretended not to see her and ran past and dared not turn his head round. Suddenly he remembered that he had to find Hall before three o'clock; where would he be? Wasn't that him there, standing on the hill by the red brick tower? Yes, surely that was him . . . And Tomas hurried on that way and climbed up the slope and Hall was waving to him; but when he got there he saw it was the brick merchant. It was too late to turn round. The brick merchant came towards him with a friendly expression, shook his hand and started to complain about the many losses he'd suffered recently. "I'm sorry," said Tomas, "but I am in rather a hurry; I'm just going in here to buy a pair of gloves." And he pushed open a heavy iron door that creaked on its rusty hinges and went into the tower. It actually was a shop selling gloves inside; Tomas himself was surprised, since the gloves were just a pretext to get away from the brick merchant. "I'd like to buy a pair of red gloves," he said, noticing, at that very moment, that it was Ellen standing behind the counter. "I only sell black gloves nowadays," she said with an apologetic smile, "because I'm in mourning. I got married yesterday." "Oh, I see," answered Tomas, in the hushed voice that goes with condolence. "My husband is very kind," Ellen continued, "and he really does love me; but he's a hunchback." Suddenly Tomas noticed that Ellen had no dress on; she was standing there in her corset, her arms bare. His blood rose; with one leap he was over the counter and holding her tight in his arms and beginning to kiss her arms and neck. "No," she said, with a shy, helpless glance, "no, I told you, I'm in mourning!" Tomas released her, against his will, but feeling he had to. She really was pale, and her eyes were red with crying. And she'd grown old — he could see that now . . . how old she'd grown, so old and faded . . .

Tomas sprang up out of his sleep: someone had come into the room.

"Oh, you still sleeping? Are you crackers or are you ill?"

It was Greta.

"Mum's so worried because you didn't come home for breakfast; she asked me to check up on you. She says you were behaving so strangely yesterday evening."

Tomas yawned deeply.

"I'll be ready in a minute. I overslept. Tell her I'm on my way."

"But for heaven's sake what happened to your cheek? Did you get into a fight? You look in a bad way!"

"I fell over on the stairs and hit my head," mumbled Tomas.

"You must've been fairly well plastered . . ."

Greta rummaged around the room, found a hand towel, dipped it in water and began to wash the blood off his cheek. But the wound opened up again, and blood started to seep forth, drop after drop. Greta stood irresolute. Finally she decisively seized a newspaper, tore a broad strip off the edge, soaked it in water and then stuck it fast along the length of the graze. Then, to be safe, she took another and laid it crosswise on top of the first.

"There. Now it's right."

"Thank you," said Tomas. "Now you can be off, and I'll be along in a minute."

"Have you got a clean shirt out? It's Sunday today, the last Sunday before Christmas . . . It's just so slovenly not putting out clean clothes on Saturday night before you go to bed. But then you were pretty out of it at the time . . ."

Greta started to hunt in a clothes drawer; suddenly she burst out laughing.

"What's this we have here? A little trumpet! Where did you get hold of this? Tu-tu-tu-tooot!"

Greta put it to her lips and tooted with all her might until she could toot no more: she was choking with laughter. Then she got out a shirt, socks and underwear and put them on the bed right under Tomas's nose.

"Bye now, and be quick . . ."

In the door she paused again and said softly, in a quite different and more serious tone, "Tomas, you know what? I've found a whole new outlook on life."

"Big deal," grumbled Tomas. "Actually I didn't know you had the old one," he added, smiling.

Greta was already on the stairs.

*

Tomas lay there looking at the snow falling outside. There was no wind and the big snowflakes fell soft and white and straight, swirling no more.

So he would live, and go forth among the others as before, and graduate, the sooner the better, and become a respected man.

Maybe he too would find a new outlook on life, like Greta.

Which, in point of fact, was something he could very well do with.

But how was it he'd received no word from Marta since she left? Did she really care nothing at all for him any more?

That was an unpleasant dream . . . He had to exert himself to retrieve a mental picture of Marta as she was, without the yellow teeth and without that strange grin.

Time to get up and live, then, and begin again. How would things be in twenty years' time? 'A long life does not always a better man make, but often increases his guilt.' Oh in twenty years he'd probably just smile at it all, should he happen to think of it. Still, it had been an unpleasantly murky tale, and he'd no desire to go through it again.

The smell of clean linen hit him when he changed into his shirt; it instilled a tantalising lust for living, never mind that his whole body felt as if it had been through a mill. His head ached and his legs felt stiff as posts, and when he finally got out of bed he was like a rider who, in the midst of some rash manoeuvre, has been thrown out of the saddle and then laboriously gets back up to continue his journey on foot with aching limbs, limping, bloodied, and filthy from the muck of the way.